127
PINEHURST

DAVID COLEMAN

NFB
Buffalo, New York

NFB
<<<>>>
NFB Publishing/Amelia Press
119 Dorchester Road
Buffalo, New York 14213

For more information visit
Nfbpublishing.com

---

*I strolled all alone through a fallout zone and came out with my
soul untouched I hid in the clouded wrath of the crowd, but when
they said, "Sit down, I stood up"*
—From *Growin' Up* by Bruce Springsteen

Also by David Coleman

Rust Belt Redemption: A Tom Donovan Mystery
Two years ago Tom Donovan was a cop, working the rough and tumble streets of Buffalo's East side. One fateful night he was involved in the deaths of a Federal agent and an unarmed man

Shadow Boxing: Tom Donovan Returns
Buffalo New York Ex cop Tom Donovan is struggling with the events of his recent past, both physically and mentally, when an event from twenty two years ago captures his attention.

Souvenir: The Third Book in the Tom Donovan Series
Carolyn Krupp already has her hands full as a single mother raising a special needs child. When her brother Mark is assaulted and left for dead at the edge of a park she asks her neighbor, ex cop turned PI Tom Donovan, to look into the matter as the police seem to already have made up their minds that Mark was in the wrong place at the wrong time and Karma caught up with him.

East Side Elegy: Book Four in the Tom Donovan Series
Tom Donovan, ex-cop turned private investigator is trying to go legitimate. New business, new office, financed in part by money with dubious origins. In walks Irene Jaworski, grandmother of the dead girl he found in a garbage bin a year ago. Irene is looking for answers and closure for a case that was never solved.

ONE

MAY 28, 1988

"WHAT A MESS," Pete Straczak said to himself. The bank had sent him to check on the house that had been seized for non-payment of taxes the week before. He didn't care much for doing foreclosures; the homes had often fallen into an advanced state of disrepair or neglect. Either that or a person or family had been evicted and put out on the street with whatever belongings they could carry and he had to sort through another person's discarded life.

The house at 106 Pinehurst was of the neglected kind. He'd heard from his contact at the bank that the police and Social Services had removed a lady from the house the previous week after she had fallen several years behind on the property. Apparently she had lived there for over fifteen years, the last few as a widow. Gina, the woman at the bank, had told him almost in a whisper; "The poor gal was batshit crazy and a fall-down drunk. It's a wonder she made it that long."

He had unlocked the padlock on the front door of the small, two story house and pushed it open, pushing a musty pile of old shoes out of the way. He walked into the parlor, the light coming from the dirty windows filtering through in a gray haze. He went to turn on a light but then remembered that the electricity had been turned off the previous week. He took the flashlight off of his belt and clicked it on. The sad looking old furniture was covered with open boxes and clothing. *How could anyone live like this?* He wondered.

He moved into the dining room. There was more junk on the scratched table and a broken chair in the corner. He started to smell something else besides the must and mildew. Probably mold, he thought. It was going to cost a small fortune to make this place livable again. From the dining room he entered the kitchen and it was even worse. A cabinet door was hanging off its hinges, and the sink was full of dirty dishes. It had been a while since he'd seen something so depressing. It looked like there had been a fire on the stove, the backsplash was charred and the paint peeling off the stove top. The mold smell was even stronger here. He held his breath as he opened up the refrigerator, probably the source of the stench.

It was empty, save for a plastic tub of margarine and a bottle of mustard. Where the hell was that smell coming from? He turned around with his light and saw a door ajar. He walked over and pulled it open, a staircase descended into the basement. The smell was coming from downstairs. "Great," he said out loud.

This was the worst part of the job. He climbed down the old wooden stairs into the dark, each step protesting as he went down. He got to the bottom and banged his head on something. He saw stars for a moment and then looked up and saw an I-beam running across the center of the basement. He put his free hand up and felt his scalp, no blood at least, but he was sure he was going to have a bump. He shone the flashlight around the space. There was a washing machine that looked like it hadn't been used in years. He checked behind it for water but it was bone dry. He stepped over to the stationary tub and checked that. It was also dry and when he tried to turn the tap on it wouldn't budge, it was rusted shut. He looked around and saw a door off its hinges leading into another part of the basement. The shadows that his flashlight were casting were doing nothing to help the uneasy feeling that was growing inside him. He carefully made his way over, being careful not to trip over any junk on the floor and peered through the doorway. There it was, an old chest freezer, with a puddle of water around it and the obvious source of the stench. It was almost overpowering now. *Great,* Pete thought to himself, the old bat probably had her pet cat in there. He opened the top of the freezer, the hinges whining and looked inside.

From inside a sheet of plastic a man's eyes looked up at him. The color was completely drained from his face and his mouth hung open. Pete screamed and felt his stomach coming up. He stumbled out of the room, tripped over something and went down hard on his face. The light clattered away from him. He got to his knees and threw up. As soon as he was able, he crawled to the stairs and ran out of the house.

Two

The tennis ball whacked off the brick wall at the back of the car dealership that fronted on Genesee Street and rolled back to thirteen-year-old Mike Schultz. He had drawn a chalk strike zone on the wall and paced off the fifty-odd feet to where the pitcher's mound would be. The sky was cloudy and the air was thick with humidity that came with an impending storm.

He reared back and threw again, this time a fastball just beneath the strike zone. Mike could do this for hours, or until his arm got tired. It was better than being at home anyway. As the ball rolled back to him it hit a rock and bounced between his legs.

"Nice catch, retard," a voice said behind him. Mike turned around and looked up. Standing ten feet away, clutching Mike's tennis ball was Fat Jack Nowak.

Mike held his hands up to prompt Jack to return the ball. "I don't think so," Jack sneered. He was a year older and thirty pounds heavier than Mike. He was the neighborhood bully and always seemed to be angry about something. No one dared call him Fat Jack to his face. Jack turned around and lobbed the ball over the six foot tall fence topped with barbed wire where the dealership kept all the junked cars they used for parts.

"You fat fuck!" Mike blurted out.

Jack whirled around. "What did you say?"

Mike was both angry and scared. He could feel his hands shaking involuntarily. Part of him wanted to run but at the same time he knew he'd have to pay the piper eventually. Still it was bad enough that the old man took the belt to him on a regular basis; there was nothing he could do about that. He'd be damned if he was going to take a beat down from this asshole. He bent down and picked up a rock, about the size of a lemon from the asphalt.

"You wouldn't dare, you pussy!" Jack spat as he stepped toward Mike.

Almost without thinking Mike heaved the rock at Jack. He didn't want to hit him in the head and knock out an eye or something crazy so he aimed low on his follow through. He drove with his legs, like his little league coach had told him and put his whole body into the delivery. The rock was a blur, catching Jack square in the groin. A look of shock came across his face and then the pain reached his brain and he dropped like a sack of flour.

Mike stood there, looking at Jack and thinking that his life may be over. "Hey!" A voice called out. Mike looked towards the voice. It was the rat-face kid, Chris or something, one of Jack's henchmen, headed his way from Clover Place. Mike was cut off from the entrance to the field that lay between Genesee Street, Clover Place, Pinehurst Avenue and the dealership. Jack was starting to pull himself together and rise to his feet. Was he crying? Rat Face was almost there and looked angry. Mike had one option.

He broke into a sprint across the field towards Pinehurst. "Get him," he heard Jack rasp behind him. He didn't look back, he just put his head down and ran. He had to be careful, the field was rutted and overgrown with weeds. He was halfway across when heard Rat Face's footsteps a few yards behind him. He knew he'd never make it to the chain link fence that divided his back yard from the field. Mike heard Rat Face stumble and he found another gear and made for the brush that ran along the back of the houses on Pinehurst. There was a small opening, about two feet high and a foot wide, he dove in. He felt something rip through his jeans near his knee.

"Shit," he heard Rat Face say. Mike crawled farther in, the branches scratching his face and arms.

"Get him out of there!" Fat Jack screamed.

"Fuck you!" Rat Face replied. "There's snakes in there."

"You Pussy!" Jack shot back. He raised his voice then. "Schultz! You can't hide in there all day! And when you come out you're dead!"

Mike wasn't going to cry. He considered his situation and looked around. Were there snakes? He could already feel the mosquitos biting his face and arms. He was lying in something wet and fetid. Still, he couldn't go back the way he came. He pulled himself forward, trying to find a way through the brush. Finally, he found a space to crawl through to reach the fences on Pinehurst but there was a dark pool of standing water. In his experience, you could never tell how deep a puddle was until you were in the deepest part. He backtracked a few yards and took a different path.

"I can hear you, you faggot!" Jack was yelling. "Come on out and take the ass-kicking you've got coming!"

Mike put his head down and pulled himself through the mud and the branches for what seemed like an hour until finally he ran into a wooden fence that had to be behind one of the houses on Pinehurst. He straightened himself up and put his hands up to try to reach the top of the fence without success. He was blocked in by branches and brush which now that he was standing, seemed to be pulling him down. There was no way he would be able to move laterally either way to get to a shorter fence that he could hop. The thought of crawling back through the brush was daunting also. He tried again to reach the top of the wooden fence and failed. This time however, the board moved.

The fence was old and the wood was soft. He pried his fingers into the crack between the boards and pulled, it moved again. As quietly as he could, he moved the board away from the fence until there was an opening just wide enough for him to slip through. He was skinny and it wasn't hard. He fell to his hands and knees and tried to catch his breath. He looked around the backyard. The grass was dead and there was a rusted out lawn mower to his left. There was a shabby looking metal table and chair to his right and no sign of any kid stuff. He had a good idea where he was. Sure enough, as he looked towards the back of the house, she was at the back door looking back at him through the ripped screen. It was the lady the neighborhood kids called Juicy Lucy, in an old bathrobe holding a cigarette.

THREE
May 28, 1988

Detective Carl Wisniewski stepped out of the front door and lit a cigarette. Six months from retirement and he had caught a stiff in a freezer. It was going to mean tons of paperwork, interviews and overtime just to put it to bed. The job had changed drastically in his twenty-four years with the Cheektowaga Police. When he was on patrol in the late sixties it was all about bar fights, stolen bikes and the occasional domestic. The last nine years as a detective had seen an uptick in violent crimes, drugs, scammers and other signs of the lowlife that had been creeping westward from the city into his suburb. Now this. He'd only worked two homicides in his tenure and they had both been cut and dried; a murder-suicide of a couple that had been on their radar for years and a brawl that had turned deadly at a bar on Union Road.

This one was different. The county medical examiner had come out and said he didn't know how long the deceased had been in the freezer. The lady who had lived in the house until recently was known in the neighborhood as a nasty drunk who probably weighed all of one hundred and ten pounds. A uniformed sergeant walked up to where Wisniewski was standing and held up a notebook. "Trying to get a line on the ex-husband," he said, referring to his notebook. "Left town in '84 with addresses in Florida until '86 then nothing."

That would be too easy, Carl thought. It couldn't be as simple as her ex old man in the freezer. He'd left town though and disappeared. Had he come back and pissed the old nutbag off?

"Thanks, Sarge," he said as he exhaled a plume of smoke. "Let me know if they get anything else." He stepped off the concrete step and looked up and down Pinehurst. Behind the modest, single family houses across the street, he could see and hear the traffic on the I-90 picking up for the afternoon commute. He wondered how somebody could live with the New York State Thruway running through their backyard. Most of the modest homes on the street were well taken care of. There were a few exceptions, like the house that he had just come out of. Peeling paint, weed strewn lawns. He'd seen it at his parent's house in Buffalo's East Side in the sixties. The neighborhood was changing, and not in a good way. The ripples of the area's eroding manufacturing base were starting to reach the suburbs. He was two doors down from the north end of the street where Pinehurst dead-ended at the base of the Genesee Street overpass. There was a rickety metal staircase that went up the side of the berm to a bus stop. Even from where he was standing he could see the stairs were probably ready to be ripped out. Carl loosened his tie, it was overcast and not too hot out but the humidity was making him perspire.

The Sergeant was walking back up to where he was standing. "Hey Wiz!" he said. "We've got a 10-71 near Schiller Park. They're requesting all units."

"Fantastic," Carl hissed under his breath. A moldering stiff in the basement and now a shots fired call.

Carl looked at a patrolman who was standing near the front door of the house he had just come out of. "You, hang back here and make sure nobody goes in," he barked. He turned and jogged towards his unmarked Ford. This was going to be one fucked up summer.

Four

July 16, 1976

Mike Schultz could feel the sweat on his face, stinging the scratches on his cheek and forehead. He looked down at his feet and then back at the woman. She was watching him through the ripped screen with a bored expression on her face. She took a drag on her cigarette and exhaled through the screen. Finally, she asked, "What the hell happened to you?"

Mike said nothing. He looked down at himself and saw he was covered with mud and green slime. Beyond being covered in filth he'd ripped a hole in his jeans, which his mother would give him holy Hell for. He looked back up at the lady who was now frowning. He mustered the courage to move and took a tentative step forward towards the driveway that ran up the side of the house.

"Aren't you going to fix my fence?" the lady asked.

Mike stopped in his tracks. He slowly turned around and looked at the board he had pulled off. He looked back at the lady who just raised her eyebrows and took another drag. He walked back to the fence, climbed up on the lower cross piece and tried to pull the board back into place. He exerted himself for a moment without much luck until he heard the door creak open behind him. His foot slipped and he landed on his feet. He turned around and the lady was looking at him and shaking her head. "Forget it," she said." She dropped the butt and stepped on it with her old slipper.

"Sorry," he mumbled.

She looked at him, appraising him. "That's a nasty cut you've got there," she said, gesturing to his forehead.

Mike put his dirty hand up to his forehead and touched it and could feel the warm blood. His mom was going to bitch to his father and then his father would no doubt kick his ass. "C'mon in and we'll get you cleaned up," the lady said.

Mike looked at her. "Juicy Lucy" and her husband had a bad reputation in the neighborhood. They were loud and drunk a lot. The cops had been to their house more than a few times to break up parties and/or fights. The husband was rumored to be usually unemployed or working odd hours. "Lucy" herself was seldom seen outside the house. If she was, it was either walking down Genesee Street or heading back home with a bottle from the liquor store on the corner (hence the nickname.) The thought of going inside the house was unsettling, but the thought of going home in his present state was worse. He nodded and followed her inside.

The kitchen was dirty. There were dishes in the sink and a pizza box from Case de Bella on the table. She pointed him to a chair at the table and left the room. Mike prayed that the husband wasn't home or going to arrive home anytime soon. The guy was big and mean-looking. He would have bet any money that even his old man would cut a wide berth to avoid him. You could usually hear him coming through the neighborhood in his late sixties Dodge Charger that had seen better days. He was thinking about bolting for the door when she came back into the kitchen holding a washcloth. She opened a cabinet and took out a bottle half full of a clear liquid. "This is the closest thing to antiseptic I guess," she said. She walked over to the sink and opened the bottle, put the cloth over the opening and splashed some of the liquid onto the cloth. She turned and approached Mike.

She was wearing jeans and a t-shirt that was too large to be her own. Her hair was pulled back in a messy ponytail. It was hard to tell how old she was. She carried herself like a young woman but her face looked weary. As she raised the cloth to Mike's face he could smell alcohol on the cloth and it reminded him of his old man when he got home late from work or the Elbow Room on Union Road.

"So, what brings you through my fence?"

Mike didn't know how to answer that. He didn't want to admit that he was running away from the neighborhood bully like a little pussy. She stepped back and appraised her work. "No answer to that, huh?" She tossed the cloth down on the table and looked him in the eye. "Are you some kind of Peeping Tom?" she asked and put her hands on her hips.

Mike's mouth fell open but no sound came out. He could feel himself blush.

Then she laughed, at first a soft chuckle that evolved into a full-fledged laugh. "The look on your face..." she said between laughing fits.

Mike felt his embarrassment turning into anger. Who the hell was this booze-bag to make him feel like a loser? She must have noticed because she stifled her laughter and looked down at him. "I'm sorry sweetie," she said. "I could hear the two kids on the other side of the fence."

Mike lost some of his steam and sat back in the chair. "Two against one, I would have taken off too," she added. He thought she might be trying to make him feel better but he wasn't sure. He looked up at her; she had green eyes and light brown hair. It was then that he noticed that when she was laughing and smiling, her face seemed to transform. The weariness and sadness disappeared, giving her a much younger look. All in all, he thought she might have been pretty but she looked tired, like she never slept. "Well I fixed your face but I don't know about your clothes," she said. He looked down at his ripped, muddy jeans again. His mother was going to freak out.

"I could throw them in the washer," she said. It took Mike a second for it to sink in then he realized that in order for him to accept the offer he would have to take his clothes off. He blushed again. "Oh, I get it…" she added seeming to realize his discomfort. "You're probably in a hurry. I have another idea. She reached for a pack of cigarettes and took one out. She fished a lighter out of her jeans and lit the cigarette. "C'mon outside."

Mike followed her out the back door and before he knew what was happening she had turned on the hose at the back of the house and was pointing it at him. He shook his head but didn't move. "C'mon," she laughed. "It'll just take a second."

He closed his eyes and felt the spray of cold water hit him. After the first shock of the cold wore off, the water felt great, washing off the mud and the sweat and the embarrassment of what he had been through. He felt like he could have stayed under the spray all day.

Finally she stopped. Mike opened his eyes and checked himself. He didn't look great, but it might be enough to keep him out of trouble. "There," she said. "In this weather you'll be dry in about twenty minutes."

"Thank you," Mike managed to say.

"No problem," she raised her eyebrows as though she were waiting for something. He eventually figured out what it was.

"Mike," he said.

He stood there feeling awkward for a moment and then nodded and started to walk towards the driveway. He turned to say something but nothing came out.

"Glenda," she said. Mike blinked, not comprehending. She tossed the cigarette butt out onto the dead lawn. "My name is Glenda."

"Thank you, Glenda." Mike felt himself blush all over again. He turned and hurried down the driveway.

FIVE
MAY 28, 1988

T HE CALL OUT to Schiller park had been a false alarm, a car backfiring and a jittery old resident thinking the worst. This seemed to be happening more often lately in the area where Cheektowaga butted up against the City's East Side. It wasn't just the influence from the city. The locals had seen a drop in their fortunes in recent decades, unemployment and the uptick in crime that came with it. Carl Wisniewski was agitated. He had hoped to have his initial paperwork on the Pinehurst matter filed already and gotten off the clock. Even though the shots fired call was bogus, it had still taken them over an hour to clear the scene and placate the natives. He just sat down at his desk in the squad room and pulled off his tie when he heard someone call his name.

"Carl!" He turned and saw it was the recently promoted Captain D'Agostino standing in his office doorway looking at him. "Do you have a minute?" the captain asked. Carl knew it really wasn't a question. He pulled himself out of his chair and followed the captain into his office.

D'Agostino was part of the new breed, college educated, bright, and polished. He'd come into the captain's job with the new Chief of Police, Richard "Swingin' Dick" Kopasz.. It had been said that the main goal of the new brass was to "modernize" the department. That was seldom an easy thing for the old guard like Carl.

D'Agostino took a seat behind his desk and was looking at a printout on his desk. That was another thing that Carl was still adjusting to, the necessity of the use of computers at the station. He still typed with two fingers and was struggling with the technology. Carl slowly eased himself onto a seat across from D'Agostino.

"What's your take on the Pinehurst thing?" D'Agostino asked.

Carl removed his notebook from his jacket pocket more as a prop than anything else. He flipped it open to the page that he'd made only a few rudimentary notes on. "Not much yet, Cap. Not until we get some more on the deceased and the lab guys are done at the scene."

D'Agostino looked up from his papers. "First impression?" he asked

Carl hesitated. He flipped the notebook over to the next page, which was blank. "Um...not really... Given the state of the house and not knowing the length of time the stiff was in the freezer..." He noticed D'Agostino flinch at the use of the word stiff. "Well, I'll know more when I hear back from the lab. Bill Miller went out to County Hospital to interview the lady of the house, but said they had her pretty doped up and she was just spouting gibberish." He closed the notebook and put it down on his thigh. D'Agostino was staring at him. He stared back. This prick, he thought, fifteen years younger and so cocky. He wasn't going to lose a staring contest.

"Alright," D'Agostino finally said. "I don't have to explain to you that this is priority one and I can get you anything you need to help you with this."

No, you don't need to tell me that, Carl thought. "Thanks, Captain," he managed to say.

"I'll let you get to it then," the Captain said as though he were dismissing him.

Carl got up and walked out of the Captain's office. His bar stool at Otto's was going to have to wait until he at least filed his initial report. What shit luck to catch this when he was literally counting the weeks until he put in his retirement papers. Now this guy was going to be breathing down his neck. "Fuck me," he muttered to himself.

Six

Mike Schultz stood at the bus stop at the corner of Clover and Meadow, thinking about what a crap summer it had been.

Things started off poorly when he told his father he didn't want to play baseball in the spring. He was good at it, naturally athletic, but it didn't interest him anymore. In fact he wondered if it ever had. The old man though, he was passionate about baseball and football. He seemed to be stuck in the past as far as that went. Most of the stories he told when he was drunk were about his own glory days at Bishop Timon High School. It was either that or he would be bitching about how he hated his boss at the railroad. Baseball seemed to be the last link Mike had to his childhood and, by extension, his father. That was also the end of any conversation regarding Mike going to a Catholic high school. Not that he cared, but his mother had pleaded with his father to reconsider. Mike had attended a Catholic elementary school through the fifth grade, when he was suspended for slapping a nun's hand off his head when she pulled his hair in an attempt to discipline him for laughing during morning mass. His grades were average at best and between the expense and the chance of being held back or expelled his father had decided, "He can go to public school with the rest of the dummies."

The Fourth of July was supposed to be great. It was the Bicentennial and Mike's friend, Larry Arnetto had invited him to go to the fireworks display at Town Park with his family. He was forced to stay home though at a cookout to entertain his snot-nosed cousin, Christopher, while his father and uncle got drunk on Genesee Cream Ale.

Then the Fat Jack rock to the crotch incident. Mike had laid low for a few days, but in the end he knew he couldn't hide all summer. Jack eventually caught up to him when he was making his way home from Mark Collins' house on Evergreen. Jack, the Rat Faced kid and the tall kid they called Itch had cut him off as he was riding his bike down Woodbine. Mike came home with a black eye, ripped shirt and a bent front rim. His mother couldn't understand why he couldn't stay out of trouble, his father just grunted and went down to his "workshop" in the basement.

He hated the first day of school. Even if this past summer was bad, it still felt like he was being sent to jail. It was his freshman year of high school and it was off to the "Big House," as the Freshman-Sophomore wing was referred to. Kid's smoked in the restrooms, detention was always overflowing and there was an ongoing feud between the "Jocks" and the "Heads," and you were expected to pick sides, that is if either side wanted you on their side.

He had been shocked when he went from the tiny Catholic Elementary school with its rigid discipline and general fear of the nuns who ran the place to the chaos that was Maryvale Junior High. The chaos seemed to be heightened at the High School level. Fortunately he had made two good friends from the neighborhood in Larry Arnetto and Mark Collins during sixth grade. They had helped him adjust to his new surroundings and brace himself for what was to come.

He got on the bus and took a seat towards the front. Larry got on at the next stop and sat next to him, nodding hello. They rode in silence to the next stop at Cherokee and Woodbine. Jack, Rat Face and Itch got on and walked right by him without even looking in his direction and went on to the back of the bus. Larry glanced at Mike and raised his eyebrows, Mike just shrugged. They arrived at school and the day began.

It went by pretty quickly. Textbooks were issued, expectations were laid out and the student population shuffled from room to room at the bell. Many of his fellow students seemed overly excited to be there for some inexplicable reason. They were chirping in the hallways and at lunch, laughing for no apparent reason at the dumbest things.

Finally—dismissal. Mike merged into the mob that was streaming out the main doors towards the waiting buses. He walked up to where his friend Mark Collins was standing and was about to say something when he felt the books he was carrying get pushed out from under his arm from behind. The two books and notebook fell onto the sidewalk in front of him. He turned around to see Fat Jack Nowak standing there with a satisfied smile on his face. "Pretty clumsy there Schultz."

Mike was furious. What made things worse was that everyone had stopped what they were doing and to look at the two of them. He turned around and bent over to collect his books.

Jack kicked him in the backside and Mike fell forward on his face. There was a smattering of laughter from the crowd and a girl's voice said, "Leave him alone." Mike stood up and felt the sting on his face where it had landed on the concrete. Mark had taken a step towards him but was cut off by Rat Face and Itch. A circle had formed around him and Jack and it was obvious what was expected.

"You gonna stand there and cry, faggot?" Jack laughed.

Mike raised his fists and Jack charged him. He threw a punch in the direction of Jack's head that glanced off his ear. Jack was all over him. He got Mike into a headlock and then down on the ground. Jack had Mike pinned down and freed his own right hand, then used it to start punching Mike in the face. Mike tried to free himself but Jack was too heavy. He tried to turn his head to protect his face but he could only move it so far. The crowd was yelling and cheering until the circle was broken by Mr. Clancy, one of the Gym teachers. He pulled Jack off Mike and then lifted Mike up by his shirt collar. "First day of school, huh boys?"

Mike and Jack were lead roughly to the Assistant Principal's office and seated a few chairs apart from one another. Mike could feel Jack looking at him and knew he would still have that stupid smile on his face so he didn't look back. Mr. Baker's office door opened and a sullen looking kid wearing ripped jeans and a black t-shirt came out. Mr. Baker stood in the doorway and looked at Jack and Mike.

"What do we have here, coach?" he asked.

"Fight at the bus stop," Mr. Clancy replied.

"First day?"

"That's what I said," Clancy said.

"I would ask what started it but it doesn't matter," Baker went on. "Three days in-school suspension for both of you and I'll need a note from a parent before the third day, telling me this won't be a recurring problem.

"What?" Jack said.

Baker bored into him with his dark, close-set eyes. "Unless you want me to call them…"

Mike looked at Jack whose cheeks had turned crimson. Jack closed his mouth tightly and looked down at the floor.

"Tomorrow, first period, room 102," Baker added. "Good day gentlemen."

That was it. No chance to explain or defend himself, Mike

thought. Not that he would have anyway. Why risk making it worse by whining like a little pussy. It was small comfort however that Jack was just as worried about how this would be taken at home as he was.

There were only three late buses and Mike didn't want to be anywhere near Jack, so he decided to walk home. It was a little over three miles but it was warm out and the walk helped him calm down. He walked into the house at 4:35. His parents were already seated at the dinner table. The old man insisted on his dinner being on the table promptly at 4:30 every day.

His mother's look of mild distress turned to shock when he entered the dining room.

"You're late," his father said and then looked up at Mike. "Jesus Christ!" he added, slamming his fork down. Mike stood there with his clothes in disarray and the bruises on his face burning anew.

"Michael…" his mother began.

"Now what, you little shit?" his father interrupted.

Mike tried to think of something to say but the words wouldn't form.

His father stood up. "Another fight?" he yelled. He looked Mike up and down. "Look at yourself. Do you think I bust my ass to buy you clothes so you can roll around in the dirt like some wild animal?"

"Michael," his mother interjected, "go get cleaned up and then come and eat dinner."

His father glanced at his mother and then turned back to Mike. "The hell with that," he growled. "If he can't respect the things I do for him then why should I feed his ass."

"Arthur…" his mother started.

"Arthur nothing," his father yelled. He walked up to Mike and slapped him hard across the face. "Get out of my sight!"

Mike staggered back and looked at his father. He was more angry than afraid. The old man was in a mood though so he turned and retreated. Instead of going upstairs to his room, he bolted for the front door. The air had cooled and felt good on his skin. His face still stung where the old man had struck him but he felt a sense of relief to be outside. He walked down Clover to Pinehurst and turned right towards the dead end. When he reached the end he sat down on the metal steps that lead up to the bus stop on Genesee. The sun was getting lower over the houses on the right side of the street, reflecting off the tops of the cars rushing past on I-90.

He could feel himself breathing deeply. He would go home in a few hours when the old man was in the basement, tying one on, and sneak up to his room. He'd have to eventually tell his mother about the note he needed for school but that could wait, preferably when the old man wasn't around and he could explain himself. He was tired and frustrated.

He heard someone coming down the steps from above him on Genesee Street. He moved over to his right to let whoever it was pass. The person went past him on the right. Out of the corner of his eye he saw a small dirty pair of sneakers. He glanced up just as the person stopped a few steps down and turned around. It was Glenda. She was wearing a hooded sweatshirt several sizes too large for her over a pair of faded jeans. Her hair was down and fell to her shoulders. She didn't look tired exactly but she didn't look alert and awake either. She studied Mike for a moment.

"Another rough day, huh?" she asked. She was carrying a bottle in a brown paper bag.

Mike didn't reply, he just looked back at her. She shrugged and turned to leave. She made it to the bottom of the stairs and turned around again. "Say, would you be able to help me with something?"

"Um," was all Mike could manage.

"Oh, sorry, I can see you're busy." She smiled at him. Again her face transformed into someone younger, less weary.

"What is it?" he asked.

"I need help moving something."

Mike glanced over her shoulder towards her house. He's noticed before that the rusted Charger was in the driveway. She looked at her home and seemed to pick up in his thinking. "He's not home," she said. "He won't be for a couple of weeks."

He felt some sense of obligation, she had helped him out this past summer. The fact that her husband was away made him less apprehensive but still, there was something about her that made him uneasy. She wasn't physically imposing, quite the opposite. She was petite and didn't look terribly healthy. But there was something in her eyes that suggested she might be unpredictable, even dangerous. "Sure," he said anyway. He realized he wouldn't have been able to say no.

She led him in through the front door. The first thing he noticed was that all the curtains had been drawn. It had been a beautiful day outside and he wondered if she had been closed up in the house all day. As far as he knew she didn't work or have any other family around except for the husband.

In the kitchen, she took a bottle of vodka out of the paper bag and put in on the counter. She lit a cigarette and took a flashlight out of a drawer. "It's in the basement," she said, exhaling a plume of smoke.

Great, Mike thought to himself. Got in a fight, in-school suspension and now I'm going to get murdered in this crazy lady's house. Still, he put on a brave face and followed her down the creaking wooden stairs.

Glenda pulled the chain on an overhead light, a bare sixty watt bulb in a socket. There was a washer and dryer that looked like they may or may not work and a rusty stationary tub. It smelled damp and musty, like there may have been water in the basement recently. She walked to a piece of plywood mounted on hinges that served as a doorway and pulled it open, revealing another room.

"It's in there," she said, nodding into the room. She walked ahead of Mike and pulled another chain. A light came on in the dank cramped space. There, perched on a few bricks, was a large chest freezer. The freezer was the only thing in the house that looked new.

"I had to unplug it when the basement flooded yesterday and I can't reach the cord." She said.

Mike stood and stared at the freezer for a moment not knowing what to do. Glenda walked to one end of the freezer and looked at him. "We just need to slide it out a little and I'll be able to reach it." He picked up on what she was saying and went to the other end of the freezer.

"Ready?" she asked.

Mike grabbed his end of the freezer and with some difficulty, they moved it about a foot away from the wall. Glenda found the cord and plugged the freezer in, the motor humming to life.

"Eddie decided he's going to make money butchering deer meat in the garage. The only problem is we don't have electricity in the garage so we compromised and put the freezer down here."

Eddie must be the husband, Mike realized. He just nodded like it all made perfect sense and followed her as she turned out the lights and headed upstairs.

Back in the kitchen, Glenda walked over to the counter and went into her purse. Mike was trying to think of an excuse to get on his way gracefully. He still didn't want to go home but "Juicy Lucy's" house made him feel uneasy. He stood and watched as she took a cigarette out of the pack and pulled out a wrinkled five dollar bill.

'Here," she said, holding out the bill.

Mike's first impulse was to grab the five and head to the door. He'd received an allowance when he was younger, but his father had put an end to the practice by saying that being fed and clothed was a bargain. Something stopped him though. "No, it's OK," he mumbled.

She looked at him and smiled, her face changing again. "What a gentleman," she said.

Mike felt himself blush and tried to recover. "Could I get one of those?" he asked, pointing at her cigarette.

She raised her eyebrows and then laughed. It wasn't a mocking laughter though, there was a sweetness to it. "How old are you?" she asked.

Mike thought about lying but dismissed the idea for some reason that he couldn't understand.

"Almost fourteen," he replied, standing up straighter.

She raised her eyebrows and pursed her lips. Then she picked the pack up off the counter and shook out a cigarette. She handed it to Mike and offered him her silver lighter. "I was twelve when I started," she said.

Mike was trying to act as cool as he could. He's taken one of his uncle's half smoked cigarettes out of an ashtray during the Fourth of July party and taken it out behind the garage when no one was looking. He wanted to rebel that night and it was the only thing he could think of. He'd lit the cigarette with a pack of matches he'd lifted from the kitchen and within seconds he found himself choking and retching with his hands on his knees. He remembered wondering how anyone could enjoy smoking.

Here he was again, ready to light up for reasons he didn't quite understand but the urge to rebel and be "cool" compelled him.

He lit the end of the cigarette and pulled the hot smoke into his mouth. He didn't choke or retch this time, but he felt the burn of the smoke and exhaled a little too quickly, holding the cigarette awkwardly in front of his face.

"Been smoking long?" Glenda asked, her voice slightly teasing.

"Not really." He took another drag and held it longer. He relaxed slightly and held the cigarette between his index and middle fingers, the way he'd seen his uncle do it.

"It's a bad habit," she added.

Mike nodded but said nothing. He became aware that Glenda was studying him.

"Another rough day?" she asked

He nodded again. "Got in a fight at school," he said.

She took a step forward and gently touched his cheek. "Is that where you got this?"

He realized there was probably a mark where his father had slapped him. "That was after..." his voice trailed off.

"At home?" she asked, taking her hand away.

Mike was becoming uncomfortable. He felt like this strange woman was suddenly crawling inside his head. He took another drag and looked back at her silently. She turned away and opened the vodka bottle. She poured a measure into a glass and leaned against the counter. "My old man used to hit me," she said. "One day I just said 'fuck this' and left."

Mike felt the urge to run out again. He took one more drag on the cigarette and realized there was a half inch ash that was about to fall to the floor. Then she was in front of him with a dirty ashtray in her hand. He quickly dropped the butt into the tray and looked up into her face. She looked tired again, any trace of mirth had left her face. She put the ashtray down and picked up the cigarette pack. "Well if you won't take any money then take these," she said offering the pack to Mike. "Eddie bought a carton before he went away so I have plenty."

Mike took the pack, mumbled a thank you and left.

SEVEN

JUNE 14, 1988

IT HAD BEEN two weeks since they found the stiff in the freezer and Carl Wisniewski was no closer to closing the case out than he had been on that first day other than determining the cause of death. Whomever it was had been cracked in the back of the head with a blunt object. No positive ID from the county crime lab, between freezing and thawing and the time that had passed the fingerprints had deteriorated and were unusable. Other identifiers were being looked at, dental records, eye color, scars and compared to Edward Kolb's military records. Kolb had served in the army in the early Seventies, but the information was slow to come from the Veterans Administration. There was also a rap sheet with a couple of busts for drug possession and one for assault. Nothing there to help, just the basic stats, height, weight and eye color. This of course would only work if the body did turn out to be that of "Eddie" Kolb. It had to be, Carl thought. They had gone over missing person reports from '84 to '88 and nothing else made sense. Kolb wasn't missing officially either for that matter. He had simply disappeared and nobody seemed to care enough to look for him.

"Carl," Captain D'Agostino's voice came from across the squad room. Carl turned around and saw the Captain standing in the doorway of his office. He pulled himself out of his chair, his knees creaking and walked across the room. D'Agostino entered his of-

fice and Carl followed after him. There were two other people in
the office, seated in front of the Captain's desk. Neither one stood
up as they entered. D'Agostino sat down behind his desk, ramrod
straight and opened a manila folder on the blotter in front of him.
Carl noticed that there were no other chairs in the room so he
shoved his hands in his pockets and leaned against the credenza
on the side wall.

After looking at the file in front of him for a moment, D'Agostino
looked up at the two men in front of him and then at Carl. "Detective Wisniewski, this is Jim Weathers from the Department of Veterans Affairs," D'Agostino said nodding towards the man closest to
Carl. The guy had bureaucrat written all over him, bad suit, skinny
tie, glasses and bored expression. He nodded at Carl with an air
of indifference. "And this is Rick Emory," D'Agostino indicated the
other man, "from the State Police."

What now? Carl wondered. The bureaucrat went first, "Detective
Wiz..." he hesitated and frowned at the paperwork on his lap.

"Wiśniewski," Carl helped somewhat impatiently. He could feel
D'Agostino shoot him a look.

"Yes," Weathers continued. He looked up at Carl. "I understand
you have yet to identify the body found at the Pinehurst address."

Carl looked at Weathers for a moment and then said, "That is
correct."

Weathers looked back at his file. "It's listed as the last permanent
address of one Edward Kolb."

"Yes," Carl wanted to tell the guy to just get to the point but didn't
want to risk any more dirty looks from his captain.

"Well if the remains are indeed those of Mr. Kolb we have a di-
lemma on our hands."

"And that is?"

"Mr. Kolb, or someone pretending to be Mr. Kolb, has been

drawing Veterans benefits up until this past year." Weathers said, looking back up at Carl.

Carl was thrown off. The reports he had said Eddie Kolb dropped off the grid in '86. "Kolb left the area in '84. Where were the checks being sent?" he asked.

"To the address here in Cheektowaga," Weathers answered.

Carl nodded and pursed his lips. "You guys don't do anything too quickly, do you?"

Another sharp look from D'Agostino but Carl didn't care.

"Meaning?" Weathers asked.

"Meaning, one of the reasons we haven't been able to ID the victim is we haven't been able to get Eddie Kolb's vitals from you people."

"Carl!" D'Agostino said abruptly.

"That's not my department," Weathers said peevishly. "My only focus is to see if fraud has been committed and if it has, try to recover the taxpayer's money."

Carl stared at the man for a moment. He knew anything he said now would come out wrong and further antagonize D'Agostino. As it was the captain had been rather icy towards him the last week or so.

"Maybe that's where I can help," Emory, the state cop said. He was wearing civilian clothes, khakis and a golf shirt, but everything else about him said State Trooper, the bearing, the haircut. He was smiling though, as if he didn't notice the tension in the room or didn't care. "I'm with the NYSP Crime Lab in Albany. Do you know anything about DNA?"

"I've read about it," Carl answered. D'Agostino nodded and Emory went on. "We are just getting the lab set up but we've already started using the tech in active cases. All we need is a sample from the deceased and something from the house that belonged to the victim. It could be anything as small and seemingly insignificant as a hair from a comb or an old toothbrush."

"I read the FBI's report on this," D'Agostino chimed in. "How accurate is it?"

"Ninety-nine point nine eight percent in most cases," Emory replied.

"The house—," Carl interjected, "we can't even call it a crime scene. The county lab guys have been through it and they keep telling me that any evidence has been compromised by time, dirt and cross contamination."

"Unfortunately we can't help you with that," Emory replied. "But hopefully we can get you a positive ID on the victim. I have to warn you though it may take a few weeks, that is if we do find something at the house we can use"

The room was silent for a moment. Finally D'Agostino spoke up. "Well, at this point we'll take all the help we can get." Carl felt the back of his neck get warm suddenly. "Carl, I'd like you to escort Inspector Emory and his team to the house on Pinehurst. Keep me updated and I will keep Mr. Weathers in the loop." Good, Carl thought, at least he didn't have to deal with the little prick from the VA.

Emory was on his feet first. "Thank you Captain," he said. He turned to Carl. "We're ready whenever you are, Detective."

That meant they were going now. Carl didn't dare look in D'Agostino's direction. "I'll grab my jacket and meet you in the back lot," Carl said.

This was a job that patrol could have handled, Carl thought as he waited in the late afternoon sun by his unmarked Crown Victoria. He'd been thinking about signing out and heading to Otto's for a cold one as soon as the Captain left but here he was, getting ready to escort a bunch of lab nerds to the house on Pinehurst.

"We're all set," came a voice to Carl's left. He turned and saw Inspector Emory, standing next to a white van. There was another man behind the wheel, turning the engine over. Carl flicked his cigarette into the storm drain and nodded.

Ten minutes later they had pulled up in front of the house on Pinehurst. Carl wiped the sweat off of his brow. It was hot for mid-June and it hadn't rained for a couple of weeks. To make matters worse the air conditioner in the Crown Vic was on the fritz. He pulled himself out of the ride and walked back to the State van. Emory and two other men were pulling white coveralls on. Emory looked up at Carl and smiled.

"Don't worry about that tool from the VA," he said. "I've been dealing with pricks like him since I got out of the Marines. They're all bark and no bite."

Carl smiled back and said, "That's what I figured." He looked across the dry, weed strewn lawn at the house. "I hate to sound skeptical, but I'm not sure what you're going to find in there Inspector. Between the way the lady lived and then us and the guys from County tromping all over the place, it's kind of a mess."

Emory zipped the white suit up to his chin. If he was as hot as Carl was it didn't show. There was not a drop of sweat on the man. "True, but it's worth a look." he said. "And what we're looking for is sometimes in the most unlikely of places."

"Fair enough," Carl said. He looked at the other three men. "Um... I don't have a suit."

"That's Okay," Emory said. "If you can just let us in we should be good to go."

Yep, patrol could have handled this one, Carl thought. He walked up to the front door, cut the crime scene tape with his pocket knife and undid the padlock that had been installed. He pushed the door and stood back, allowing the three men to enter with their tool boxes and space suits. He went back to the car, climbed in, turned the motor on and fired up the AC, for whatever good it would do. He looked down at the passenger seat. He'd thought to bring the file on the Pinehurst case in case the Staties had any questions but now he knew they wouldn't. He picked it up and flipped it open and started idly leafing through it. He stopped when he got to Patrol's neighborhood canvas. He'd only given it a passing glance when it first hit his desk but now who knew how long he'd be sitting there. He scanned the notes the watch sergeant had put together, names, addresses and anything that passed for interesting regarding what the woman's neighbors had recalled. All in all it wasn't much. She rarely seemed to have gone out and when she did everyone cut her a wide berth. She was sullen and kept to herself by all accounts. No complaints about loud noises or anything else in the last four years. One of the older neighbors re-called the husband being a bit of a hell raiser but that all went away when he did. Most of the neighbors had nothing to add. Patrol had done a pretty thorough job of canvasing the nearby residents. Carl was just about to flip the page when a name caught his eye. 52 Woodbine Street, Mr. Robert Czerczak, retired, Cheektowaga Police Department.

"Big Bob," Carl said to himself. Bob Czerczak had been a legend in the department. He'd put in thirty-seven years and retired in the early '70s. His career and Carl's had only overlapped for a few years and at that time Czerczak was the day shift Desk Sergeant, but the stories about him were told with reverence. He'd gone toe to toe with bikers in the town's Tiorunda neighborhood, broken up fights at the dive bars at the edge of town, he'd even been shot on duty while answering an armed robbery call. He was tall and physically intimidating, but that hid an affable nature and a wicked sense of humor. Carl looked up at the Pinehurst house. No telling how long the lab geeks were going to be in there and Big Bob was right around the corner. Maybe he had some insight into the case or maybe he didn't. Carl decided to take the short walk and pay his respects.

EIGHT

DECEMBER 20, 1976

IT WAS THE first day of Christmas vacation. It had been pretty quiet at the Schultz house for the last few months. Mike had managed to stay out of trouble since his suspension and was pulling mostly B grades with minimal effort. Still his father rarely spoke to him, but that was okay with Mike. His mother on the other hand, seemed to be going out of her way to be nice to him, but only if the old man wasn't around.

Larry Arnetto had been shooting his mouth off on the bus home the day before, going on about how good their street hockey team was. They'd beaten a couple of teams from Chapel Avenue and Wellworth Place handily. Fat Jack had listened and issued a challenge. "We could kick your faggot asses," he'd said. Larry wouldn't back down and a game was set for this afternoon. A neutral spot on Woodbine Avenue was chosen.

Mark Collins was already there, assembling the makeshift nets that his father had made out of spare two by fours and chicken wire. "Hey," Mike said walking up to Mark.

"Hi," Mark responded. "Everybody's coming." Mark was the unofficial captain and general manager of the team. He was the best athlete of the group, already having made the freshmen basketball team at school as well as just having finished the Freshman football season. That would mean that Larry, Dan Torlone, and Tim Burns were on their way. There was one problem though.

"What about Rick?" Mike asked. Rick Petrowski was a stalwart on defense. The problem was he'd broken his arm while riding his bike in the creek behind the apartments on George Urban Boulevard.

"Larry's bringing his cousin Nick," Mark replied.

"Who?"

"Larry said he can play. He's fourteen and just moved into the neighborhood."

"I hope he's better than Larry," Mike responded.

It was cold, below freezing, the ground was hard but it hadn't snowed so the street was clear. The perfect conditions for street hockey. Larry arrived with his cousin Nick. Nick was short but stocky and had long unkempt hair. He nodded at Mike and Mark while being introduced. Dan and Tim arrived shortly after pulling an old Courier Express wagon that Tim used to carry his home made goalie pads and other equipment.

A few minutes later Jack arrived with the rest of his team from Cherokee Avenue, Itch, the rat- faced kid and three others whom Mike recognized from the bus. One of them had to be Rat Face's little brother, a smaller version of him with the same rodent like features. It took a few minutes for them to help Rat Face the Younger put on his makeshift goalie equipment but then the game was underway.

It only took a few minutes for it to become clear that Mike's team was superior. Young Rat Face was terrified of the hard plastic street hockey ball and gave up two easy goals. Added to that it looked like no one on Jack's team had played much street hockey at all, let alone as a team. Mike, Mark and Dan worked together as a unit, passing the ball back and forth to the open man and keeping constant pressure on the other team's defense. After the fourth unanswered goal, Jack was red-faced and angry. "Marty," he snapped at one of his teammates, "you play forward and I'll go back on defense."

Play resumed and it was much the same. At one point, Mike lifted Marty's stick and stole the ball from behind him. Mark saw what was happening and turned up the street towards the other team's goal. Mike hit his stride with a perfect pass. There was only one man back. It was Jack. Before Jack knew what happened, Mark had put the ball between his legs and was stepping around Jack for a clean breakaway on goal. Jack, knowing he was beat, turned around and slashed Mark hard on the ankle as he was going by him.

Mark grunted and went down hard on his side. He rolled over, clutching his ankle. Without thinking Mike dropped his stick and ran up to Jack. "You fat fuck!" he screamed.

Jack glared at Mike, his stick still in his hand. "What are you going to do about it pussy?" he sneered.

Out of the corner of his eye, something flashed by Mike. It was Larry's cousin Nick. He left his feet and unleashed a vicious cross check on the side of Jack's head. Jack tumbled to the ground with Nick on top of him. Jack probably had twenty pounds on Nick but Nick had a knee on Jack's chest and was firing punches at Jack's head. Jack for his part could only try to cover up. Nick had a wild look in his eye that was disconcerting. Rat Face ran up and tried to pull Nick off, but Mike grabbed him and put him in a headlock. Rat Face was cursing and struggling to get free, but Mike felt a surge of adrenaline kick in and held on tighter than he knew he could.

Mark was back on his feet and was squared up with Itch, his fist cocked, ready to go. Itch didn't seem to be interested in fighting though. He couldn't seem to take his eyes off of the ass-kicking Fat Jack was getting.

"Nicky, Jesus Christ!" Larry yelled at his cousin. Nick didn't stop though, if anything his attack intensified. Mike had never seen anything like it. Nick had obviously beaten the fight out of Jack but he showed no signs of stopping. Jack's nose was bloodied and he had a cut on his cheek.

"Hey!" a voice came from off to the side. Mike looked up and saw that a man was coming down the driveway of the house on the corner. Mike didn't know his name but knew he was a retired cop. His house was on the corner directly across the street from Mike's and Mike's father had complained several times about the man not minding his own business.

"Knock it off!" the man said advancing towards the fracas. He pulled Nick up by his collar and then put him in a bear hug. He had to be in his sixties, but he was big and physically imposing. Nick stopped struggling and then the man let him go. "You little bastards take this shit somewhere else," he growled.

The game was over. Jack got to his feet, his face bloodied and his jacket ripped. He was clearly crying. Without a word he and his team walked away towards Cherokee.

"Damn," Tim said, his goalie mask in his hands.

Mark limped up to Nick and held out his hand. "Thanks," he said.

Nick shrugged and shook Mark's hand. Even though the madness had gone out of his eyes, they still had a mischievous look to them. "Fuck that fat ass," he said with a smile.

Everyone had packed up to leave. Mike was helping Mark disassemble the nets.

"That kid is crazy," Mark said, obviously referring to Nick.

Mike thought for a moment and then said, "Yeah, but you can't say Jack didn't have it coming."

Mark just gave Mike an odd look and went back to work. Just then it started to snow.

NINE

JUNE 14, 1988

CARL WALKED THE half block South on Pinehurst and turned left onto Clover Place. For mid-June it was hot and dry, the people who bothered maintaining their lawns were already fighting an uphill battle. The grass was turning brown and the weeds were the only thing that seemed to be thriving. He was sweating through his shirt and wondered if he could even come close to passing the department's fitness test. As a twenty-plus year veteran and a detective he was exempt from the yearly fitness test that the rank and file had to undergo. The department had changed too; the days of the stereotype fat beat cop at the donut shop were over. The young guys all looked like football players now. Carl had to admit to himself that the change was probably necessary, the town had changed as well.

He walked up to the house on the corner, Bob Czerczak's house. Big Bob had been the farthest thing from the donut-munching stereotype that there was. Even though Czerczak had served in a simpler time, or so it seemed, his dedication and fearlessness were legendary. There hadn't been a barroom brawl or armed robbery or domestic call that Czerczak hadn't been able to walk into and diffuse, by force if necessary. His methods would probably be frowned upon today, Carl thought. He would seldom wait for backup and had cracked more than one skull with a leather blackjack that he kept on his belt. His methods had almost gotten him killed once. An armed robber shot Czerczak three times when he was the first responding unit at a liquor store robbery on Kensington Avenue. But then again that story was a part of the "Big Bob" mystique; he had returned fire and wounded his assailant. The robber was found dead in a stolen car later that day, with a blood-stained bag of cash on the seat beside him. It had happened before Carl had joined the CPD but he had seen it on the news. He remembered how the whole area was shocked that violent crime had spread from the city to the peaceful suburbs.

Czerczak's house was on the corner of Clover and Woodbine but the driveway was on Woodbine. As Carl approached the one story brick house he noticed it was starting to show signs of neglect, peeling paint, a rusty aluminum awning over the front porch. The driveway was empty but there was a single car garage attached to the house. He walked up to the front door and rang the bell.

Nothing at first. There was no light behind the small rectangular window on the front door and the curtains were drawn in the front window. He thought he could hear voices, maybe from a TV. He waited a moment and then turned to walk back off the porch. Just as he did, he heard the door open behind him. He turned and saw an old man looking back at him. The man was tall and he was squinting. Even though Carl had not laid eyes on him in over ten years he recognized Big Bob Czerczak.

With some effort Czerczak pushed open the storm door and looked at Carl. "Can I help you?" he said. Carl noticed that the left side of Czerczak's face didn't seem to move as he spoke.

Carl decided against flashing his badge, he had hoped to keep this visit unofficial. "Bob Czerczak?" he asked.

Czerczak stared at him for a minute and then smiled a lopsided smile. "Carl Wisniewski…" He looked Carl up and down. "What are you? A detective or something?"

"Yep," Carl replied.

"Will wonders never cease?" Czerczak said. "Come on in and have a beer."

Carl reluctantly declined the offer of a cold beer; he didn't want the State Police techs he was escorting making any noise. He accepted a glass of water and watched while Czerczak opened a bottle of Genny using his one good arm and the crook of his other arm. He explained to Carl that he had suffered a stroke two years before. He was still going to physical therapy once a week but he had probably regained as much mobility as he was going to. Czerczak had no family around to speak of. His wife Patty had died of ovarian cancer in '79 and his only son had made a career out of the Navy and was now stationed in San Diego with a family of his own. "I tell him I'm fine," Czerczak said of his son. "He's got enough on his mind without worrying about me." Czerczak glanced at the table next to his chair. There was a photo of a much younger version of himself and his late wife next to a photo of him and his son in fishing gear.

"What about you?" Czerczak asked. "Sorry, I can't remember... do you have kids?"

Carl shook his head. "No, we never did, we couldn't." he said. He decided not to tell him that he and Margery had been divorced for eight years.

Carl knew he didn't have all night. He felt bad, finding Czerczak, a shell of his former self, living in a stuffy little house all by himself, but he hadn't told the State guys he was leaving and decided to get to the matter at hand.

"I guess you heard about the body we found around the corner?" Carl asked.

Czerczak nodded. "Yeah, I did. Some wet behind the ear patrolman came knocking on the door the day after you found it."

"I saw your name on the canvas report, did he take a statement?"

Czerczak shook his head this time. He said, "Nothing to tell him really. I knew the couple that lived there but that was about it. The guy was a real shit-bird and the wife was a recluse. Other than that there's not too much I can tell ya."

Carl could picture the patrolman going through the motions while conducting the neighborhood canvas. He'd done the same thing once or twice when he was younger. He looked at Big Bob now and wondered if there was anything else the ex-cop could offer.

"So you knew Eddie Kolb?" Carl asked.

"Who?" Bob asked squinting.

"The guy who lived at 127 Pinehurst."

"Yeah, that guy. I knew him by sight. They moved in the year after I retired. Loud muscle car, parties, a bunch of sketchy people driving through the neighborhood at odd hours."

"Sketchy people?"

"If I had to guess," Bob said, "I'd say they were selling drugs at the house. But I was off the force by then and Patty was always telling me to mind my own business and stop thinking like a cop." He smiled a crooked smile at the memory of his wife.

"Do you think It was him?" Carl asked. "In the freezer?"

"Wouldn't be surprised," Bob answered. "He was a scumbag and that sounds like a scumbag way to go."

Carl thought for a moment and then asked, "What about the wife?"

"What about her?"

"Is she my perp?"

Bob shook his head. "Doubt it," he said. "She was a squirrelly thing to be sure, but she probably weighed a buck-ten soaking wet. That Kolb guy was a big fucker and I can't see her taking him down and stuffing him in a freezer."

"Unless she had help," Carl offered.

"I suppose."

"Anybody else you think we should be looking at?"

"I don't know…" Bob took a sip of his beer. "There were some of the neighborhood kids who were always hanging around that end of the street. If you ask me, Kolb was a blight on the neighborhood and society in general."

"Do you have any names?"

"Nah, just some neighborhood rats with too much time on their hands."

Carl knew he had to get back to the house on Pinehurst and the lab crew. He stood up and thanked Bob for his time.

"No problem," Bob said. "It's been a while since I talked shop with anybody." He laboriously pulled himself out of his chair and shook Carl's hand.

There was an awkward silence for a moment and then Carl said, "Take care of yourself Bob. If you ever need anything just call the station and ask for me." He felt a pang of guilt saying this knowing that in a few months he wouldn't be there to take the call.

"Will do… Detective," Bob answered with a mock salute.

As Carl walked back to the house on Pinehurst he thought of the things that Czerczak had said and was starting to wonder if the old man was holding something back. He dismissed it as paranoia, probably due to the stalled nature of the case. As he was walking up the driveway of the house he noticed the techs had opened the door of the dilapidated garage at the back of the property. There was an old Dodge Charger that was covered with dust and grime.

"There you are," It was Emory, the lead tech walking towards Carl from the front of the house."

"Sorry," Carl offered. "I was following up on a canvas interview."

"No problem," Emory said. "Not much going on in the house but one of my guys found this in the car." He held up a plastic evidence bag. Carl squinted at it. It looked like a rag with a copper colored stain.

"What is it? Carl asked.

"It's a hand towel with what appears to be quite a bit of blood on it," Emory answered. "If It's Kolb's we can try to match it with some of the effects he left behind as well as the unfortunate soul from the basement."

TEN

CHRISTMAS BREAK HAD come and gone. Mike had indulged his mother and attended Midnight mass at Our Lady Help of Christians on Christmas Eve. His father was absent, claiming he was exhausted from the double shift he had worked at the railyard the day before. Mike's Mother still attended Sunday Mass regularly but Mike and his father went less and less frequently. Mike knew this bothered his mother, but the older he got the more he questioned what all of the ritual and rote memorization that represented Catholicism to him really was accomplishing. He wasn't sure if there was a God, but he had his doubts that he existed inside the stuffy walls of the church.

Christmas day went by without incident. His mother was up early, fussing over breakfast and when Mike and his father came downstairs, presents were opened and even his father seemed to be in a good mood. Later that day, his uncle, aunt and cousins came over and stayed too long. All in all though, it wasn't that bad.

School resumed and the routine began again. There were a few differences though. Jack Nowak sat near the front of the bus with his gang, cutting Mike, Mark, Larry and especially Nick Arnetto a wide berth. Mike had found out that Nick had previously attended school in Depew but his parents had split up and his father had moved into an upper flat on Meadow Place, around the corner from Clover. While Mike was grateful to Nick for giving Fat

Jack the beat- down he had coming, something about Nick made him uneasy. He knew Mark Collins felt the same way, maybe even more so. Mark went out of his way to avoid Larry when he was in the presence of his cousin Nick.

It had started to look like it was going to be a rough winter. Temperatures were in the twenties and there were a couple of bad storms. There was at least a foot of snow on the ground by the last week of January. The worst was yet to come however.

That Friday all Hell broke loose. School was let out early and the bus home inched its way down Union Road and then Genesee Street in white-out conditions. The temperature had dropped below zero and by the time Mike had trudged his way home from the bus stop his face was raw and he had lost feeling in his fingers. He hadn't seen fit to wear a hat or gloves lest he look like a little kid and now he was paying the price. His mother met him at the door and took him into the kitchen to run cool water over his hands until the feeling returned. He noticed she looked worried.

"I haven't heard from your father and the news said it's going to get worse," she said.

How much worse could it get, Mike wondered.

His father finally called after four o'clock, saying he was stuck at the railyard at the Central Terminal. He was going to ride out the storm in the signal house with two co-workers. He had considered trying to come home but a radio report had said that there were cars stuck on the Skyway and the thruway and traffic was at a standstill everywhere.

All that night the wind howled, making the windows rattle and the roof creak. Mike went upstairs and tried to go to sleep but he could hear the television downstairs, his mother glued to the news for any updates. The wind chill had dropped to -40, making it dangerous to go outside.

Mike woke in the morning to the sound of the phone ringing downstairs. He heard his mother answer but could barely make out the muffled strains of her side of the conversation. He had just rolled over and tried to go back to sleep when he heard his bedroom door open.

"Michael," his mother said.

He rolled over and looked at his mother, standing in the doorway in her bathrobe with her hair up in rollers.

"Your father just called; he's going to try to make it home and wants you to shovel the driveway."

Mike didn't protest. His mother looked exhausted and probably had been up most of the night worrying. "Make sure you bundle up. It's still below freezing outside," she added and then turned and left.

Mike dressed in layers, jeans over his pajama bottoms, two pairs of socks and two sweatshirts. He went downstairs where his mother met him with gloves, scarf, a hat and a pair of his father's old work boots. The shortest path to the garage was the kitchen door at the rear of the house. He opened the door and found that the snow had drifted about half way up the storm door. He tried to push the storm door outward but it wouldn't budge. He and his mother went to the front door and it was also blocked but not as badly. With some effort he forced the door open and stepped out onto the front stoop.

The wind ripped at his face and he pulled the hood of his parka down to block it. When he did look up everything was white. Snow had blown and drifted up the entire sides of the houses up and down the street and there wasn't a sign of life. It looked as though the town highway department had plowed at some point during the night but the snow had continued and blown back into Clover Place. He wondered if his father would be able to get down the street even if he made it back to Cheektowaga. Fortunately, much of the snow had blown out of the driveway and he was able to trudge back to the garage with minimal difficulty. He tried the garage door but the handle seemed to be frozen solid. He walked around to the side of the garage and was able to shoulder his way through the man-door and retrieve the shovel.

His feet and hands were already cold by the time he walked to the street end of the driveway. Even though all but a foot of snow had drifted off a main portion of the drive, there was a three foot drift at the street end that had to be contended with.

He set to work and the exertion helped the blood flow return to his extremities. He found that shoveling the snow to his right was better, the wind catching it and tossing it off to the side. He worked quickly and after a short time had cleared the drift. His face was stinging and his nose was running as he turned to work his way up to the rest of the driveway. He considered packing it in briefly and then realized he didn't want to give the old man something else to bitch about. Working between his house and the neighbors seemed to cut down on the wind a bit and he was able to finish the driveway in about thirty minutes. He looked down towards the street and saw that snow had drifted back into the foot of the drive but not enough to keep the old man's Chevy Impala from making it in. He returned the shovel to its place in the garage and headed towards the back door of the house.

He paused at the door, a thought occurred to him. He found himself wondering about the woman on Pinehurst. Was it any of his business? No, but her husband's car had still been sitting idle in the driveway whenever he had walked past the house and he might still be away. His curiosity got the better of him and he walked towards the street. Across the way, the old guy who had broken up the fight at the street hockey game was out shoveling his driveway.

Mike trudged his way around the corner onto Pinehurst and made his way down the street. As he approached Glenda's house he noticed it was dark, not that that was unusual, but it looked even more forlorn than usual. There were icicles hanging from the eaves and snow drifted up to the front door. The car was there in the driveway, mostly covered with snow and one of the front tires looked to be flat. He walked up the driveway, skirting the snow that had drifted up the side of the house and made his way to the back door.

The glass had fallen out of the storm door and he reached through and knocked on the wood door behind it and waited. No response. He looked through the frost covered glass into the darkened kitchen and saw no movement. Had she gone out? The snow around his feet seemed undisturbed by footprints. Also, Glenda very seldom left the house, unless it was to go to the corner market or the liquor store. He knocked again and waited. He stepped back off of the concrete stoop and considered going home. The wind was cutting through the layers of clothes he had on and he was exhausted from shoveling.

His curiosity got the better of him and he stepped back up to the door, reached through the opening and pushed at the door. Sure enough, the door creaked open. He wrenched the storm door outward and stepped inside.

"Hello," he said in a voice that was loud enough to be heard without startling anyone. No answer. He closed the back door and immediately realized that the warmth he had anticipated from coming inside was not there. He could still see his own breath.

"Hello," he said again, louder this time. He entered the living room and it was dark as well. Glenda's coat was on a hook by the front door and a pair of boots was on a mat below it. He checked the downstairs bathroom and it was empty. He returned to the living room and peered up the stairs. The whole house was eerily quiet with the exception of the wind gusts rattling the windows occasionally. Mike quietly ascended the stairs. In the hallway he looked into another empty bathroom and then an unfurnished bedroom to his right. One last door to his right and he stepped over and slowly pushed it open.

She was on the bed, covered with multiple blankets and a knit hat on her head. Mike thought she might be dead until he stepped forward close enough to hear her breathing unevenly. There was a bottle of pills and near empty bottle of vodka on the nightstand. Mike was starting to panic. Had he walked in on a suicide attempt? Or had she just passed out while trying to ride out the storm. In any event, the furnace was obviously not working and he knew that he couldn't leave her like this.

"Glenda," he said, tapping her on the shoulder. She mumbled something and opened her eyes.

"Glenda, it's Mike Schultz" he said. She looked up at him without any sign of recognition and mumbled again.

"What's wrong with the furnace?" he asked.

"F... broken," was all he could make out from her response.

"Glenda, I'm going to call an ambulance," Mike said, trying to hide the panic in his voice.

"No!" It was her first response that he understood clearly.

"What? You can't stay here like this."

"No ambulance or cops!" she responded, her agitation rising through the fog.

Mike thought he understood. He had previously pieced together that Glenda's husband, Eddie might have gone to jail while he was "away."

Mike thought about what he should do. His mother was one option but she would naturally wonder what Mike was doing in this strange lady's home. The retired cop? Mike knew that the man and his dad didn't get along and he probably thought Mike was some kind of punk after the street hockey incident, but who else could he go to?

"I'll be back," he said. He didn't wait for a response. He left the room and ran down the stairs and out the back door.

He trudged around the corner and saw the retired cop still working diligently on his driveway. He was about ten feet away when the man looked up and saw him. The man pulled down the scarf wrapped around the bottom of his face and looked at Mike with cold, blue eyes. "Can I help you?" he asked.

Mike stood for a moment. He hadn't thought about what he'd say and now found himself at a total loss as how to explain the situation to an adult, let alone a retired cop.

"What's the matter son?" the man said. "It's too cold for a staring contest."

"The lady..." Mike began.

"What lady?" the man asked, growing impatient.

"On Pinehurst. She's sick and her heater's not working."

"What lady on Pinehurst?"

"Her name is Glenda and she lives at 127."

"How do you know all this?" the man asked.

Mike was ready with a lie faster than he imagined he could be. "She hired me to shovel her driveway when I went in to get paid I found her.

The man looked at Mike like as if he suspected that there were holes in his story but finally said, "Wait here, I'll grab my tool box."

A few minutes later, Mike led the man back to the house on Pinehurst. As soon as they entered the back door the man opened his tool box and took out a flashlight. "I'll check the furnace," he said. He found the door to the basement and went downstairs.

Mike went back upstairs to check on Glenda. She was either asleep or passed out again. Mike double checked to make sure she was still breathing and she was. He paused and thought for a moment. The man in the basement was bound to ask questions that he was ill-prepared to answer and in her current state Glenda was going to be no help. Still, he knew he had respected her wishes so far. He pulled the covers up to her chin and turned to leave.

The man was standing in the bedroom door with a concerned look on his face. "The pilot light was out," he said, looking past Mike at the figure on the bed. His eyes then went to the nightstand. "Jesus," he said.

Eleven

June 16, 1988

It was time to take another run at interviewing Glenda Kolb. Bill Miller, who had recently been promoted to detective when the department decided to expand the squad from six to eight, had been seconded to the case with Carl. Miller had attempted an interview with her but had claimed she was incoherent at the time. Miller was at least 15 years younger than Carl and had an energy and enthusiasm that annoyed Carl. Fortunately, at first for Carl, Miller had his own caseload to contend with and therefore had stayed out of Carl's business for the most part. Captain D'Agostino was getting impatient though and insisted that Miller and Carl start working on the Pinehurst case full time, together. That meant they would be going out to the County Home in Alden together to take another run at Glenda Kolb.

It was a half hour ride in the town issued Crown Victoria. Neither man said much. At one point Miller turned the car's radio up during some hair band's song. He glanced over at Carl and picking up on the sour look on Carl's face, turned the volume down.

It had been a while since Carl had been to the County Home. It was where the area's indigent wound up when the other hospitals and homes wanted to rid themselves of the people who couldn't afford private healthcare. It was a hot, hazy day, the sun beating down on the pavement on Route 33. It felt more like late July than mid-June. Carl couldn't remember the last time it rained.

They arrived at the home just after noon. They entered the dingy foyer and badged the security guard at the front desk and asked for Glenda Kolb. The guard, who looked bored to the point of being unconscious, checked a clipboard and pulled out two visitor passes. "Third floor, Ward E," he said and went back to his newspaper.

The elevator was out of service so they took the stairs. If the building's air conditioning was on it wasn't doing a very good job, Carl was sweating through his shirt under his sport coat. They followed the sign to Ward E and walked up to an unattended nurses' station. Someone, a patient, was screaming from a room down the hall. The air smelled of disinfectant trying vainly to cover up the stench of human waste.

"Where is everybody?" Carl asked no one in particular.

Miller looked at his watch. "At Lunch?" he offered.

Carl grunted and started off down the corridor with Miller in his wake. An orderly with a cart full of cafeteria trays entered the hallway and almost bumped into Carl.

"We're looking for Glenda Kolb," Carl said holding up his badge.

The orderly looked confused for a moment but then said. "Oh yeah" he gestured over his shoulder. "Room 314." He started down the hall towards the nurses' station and added, "Good luck."

Carl looked at Miller who shrugged in return. They walked another thirty feet until they came to room 314. There were two beds in the room, the one closest to the door occupied by an elderly black woman eating Jell-O. Carl looked at the other bed and knew something was wrong.

"Fuck," he said louder than he intended to.

"What?" Miller asked.

"That's not Glenda Kolb."

Miller frowned. "That's the lady I tried to talk to last week," he offered.

Carl shook his head. "Glenda Kolb is listed at thirty five years of age." He turned to face Miller.

"How old do you think that lady is?"

Miller looked slack jawed at the woman in the far bed. Even if Glenda Kolb had led the hard life people had described there was no way that the old woman he looked at now was a day under sixty.

TWO HOURS LATER, Carl and Miller were standing in front of Captain D'Agostino's desk. D'Agostino was looking up at them expectantly with his brow furrowed. "Who is she?" he asked. "And better yet, where the hell is Glenda Kolb?"

Carl glanced at Miller who was looking back at D'Agostino with his mouth drawn tight. Obviously, he was going to be no help at the moment.

"We spent an hour in the administrator's office trying to sort it out, Cap," Carl offered. "To the best of their recollection, she is the person removed from the house on Pinehurst. The paramedics took her to County when they couldn't find anywhere else to take her."

D'Agostino shook his head, "And they just admitted her without any ID?" he asked.

"Apparently the deputy who handled the eviction couldn't find anything in the house except for a pile of overdue bills with Glenda Kolb's name on them and he just assumed..." Carl answered with a shrug.

"Sweet Jesus," D'Agostino moaned. He looked directly at Miller. "And you didn't pick up on any of this?"

"Well..." Miller coughed and then continued. "When I went out there last week all I had was a name. I tried to talk to the lady but she is practically catatonic."

D'Agostino rocked back in his chair and rubbed his temples. He let out a long breath and then stood up. "Okay, Bill, go back to the house and look for anything, I mean anything that will tell us who this person is or where the Hell Glenda Kolb has gotten off to." Carl could see Miller shuffling his feet anxiously until D'Agostino stared him into being still. "Try not to come back empty handed. Carl, re-interview the neighbors, the whole damn street if you have to and find out what the fuck is going on."

Carl nodded. He'd never heard the Captain curse before and thought it best if he just got out of his sight for the time being. The two detectives shuffled out of D'Agostino's office.

TWELVE

Bob Czerczak gestured for Mike to follow him downstairs after Glenda closed her eyes and seemed to go back to sleep. "We should probably get some food in her," he said. See if there is anything in the cabinets. After a short search Mike found a can of soup. Bob found a grungy looking can opener and proceeded to heat up the soup in a small pan he had located under the counter. Mike stood off to the side. He could feel the kitchen getting warmer, the furnace clunking away in the basement.

"See if you can find a bowl or a mug," Bob said over his shoulder. Mike looked through the cabinet where he had seen Glenda keep her glassware and found an old, chipped coffee mug.

He turned and saw that Bob was looking at him. Mike handed him the mug.

"Are you going to tell me why you were really in this lady's house," Bob asked.

Mike looked down at the floor. He knew his story had holes in it.

Bob shook his head. "I mean, it's a good thing you were," he said in a calmer tone. "Who knows what would have happened if you didn't find her."

Mike looked up. "I met her last summer," he said. "I guess I was worried about her."

"Why?"

Mike shrugged. He didn't know how to explain Glenda to the old cop.

"How well do you know these people?" Bob pressed.

"Not that well I guess. I've never met her husband."

"So where's the husband?"

"I dunno," Mike shrugged. "She just said he's away."

Bob frowned. "Listen kid, I don't know anything about the girl upstairs but I gotta tell you I got a bad feeling about the husband. I've dealt with guys like him my entire life."

Mike just looked at Bob, not knowing what to say.

Bob poured the soup into the mug. He went on, "You did the right thing today. Just be careful who you get involved with. That's all I'm saying."

Mike nodded and Bob handed the mug and a spoon to him. "I'm going to go home now. The furnace is on again. Try to get her to eat this but don't stay too long. I'm sure your folks will be worried about you.

"Yes sir," Mike replied.

He watched Bob pull his coat on, pick up his tool box and go out through the back door. It was snowing again. He'd have to check on Glenda and probably go home and shovel again before his father got home.

Thirteen

June 20, 1988

Carl's first attempt to answer the phone on his nightstand ended badly. He had swung his arm and knocked the phone off the table next to his bed and it clattered to the floor. His head was pounding and his mouth was dry. He painfully tilted his head to the side to look at the alarm clock. It was 9:15 AM.

He heard a tinny voice coming over the phone receiver on the floor next to his bed. His stomach lurched as he rolled over to reach down and pick it up. "Carl?" he heard the voice say.

"Yeah," his voice rasped as he put it to his ear.

"Where are you buddy?" It was Bill Miller. Stupid question as Miller had called him at home.

"Wassup," Carl asked sitting up. He had stayed at the Barracinni's longer than he had intended, trying to chat up a divorcee but in the end going home alone.

"You'd better haul ass and get in here," Miller responded. "'Dago-stino' is looking for you (a nickname that no one dreamed of using within the Captain's earshot). We have a meeting with the Chief at 10 o'clock sharp."

"On my way," Carl said and slammed the phone down. "Fuck," he said to himself. He could still taste the cigarettes and whiskey from last night. He pulled himself out of bed and headed towards the bathroom.

He made it to the station just before ten. He picked up his notes, checked his breath and headed down the corridor towards the Chief's office. The Chief's secretary Angela nodded for him to go through the double doors into the office and he quietly let himself in.

The conference table in the Chief's suite was almost full. He tried to avoid making eye contact with D'Agostino but could almost feel the disapproving stare the Captain shot his way. He looked towards the head of the table where Chief Kopasz was sitting, looking intently at a printout on the table in front of him.

"Detective, nice of you to join us," Kopasz said, finally looking up. Carl felt his neck get hot as he sat down at the last open chair at the far end of the table. Kopasz wasn't an in-house hire like the previous CPD chiefs had been. He had spent twenty years rising through the ranks of the Erie County Sheriff's Department. He'd put enough time in to retire, but the town board, in an effort to "shake things up," had reached outside the department and persuaded Kopasz to take the job.

"Where is Miller?" Kopasz asked looking directly at Carl.

Before Carl had to admit that he had no clue where Bill Miller was, D'Agostino spoke up, "He's interviewing a neighbor of the Kolb's who'd been out of town for the past two weeks."

"Okay then let's get started," the chief said. Carl looked around the table. In addition to Kopasz and D'Agostino, he recognized Rick Emory from the State Police lab and one of his crew to his right. Across the table, he thought he recognized a guy from the county medical examiner's office seated next to a man he didn't know.

"Still no ID on the woman at the County Home?" the chief asked.

Carl cleared his throat, "No sir, the doctor there said she is still not answering any questions. She's responsive and seems to be aware of her surroundings but she hasn't said a word."

The chief shook his head, "God dammit, how is it that in this day and age somebody just drops out of the sky and we can't find out who she is?" He looked at Carl again. "And we still have no idea where Glenda Kolb is?"

"No sir," Carl responded, trying to keep his tone neutral. He didn't want to sound whiney or defensive in front of the chief. He knew, to guys like Kopasz, those were signs of weakness.

"Right," Kopasz went on. "Inspector Emory, I understand you have more bad news?'

Emory, unflappable as always, looked back at the chief and spoke, "We found enough of a sample from the car to rule out that the body in the freezer was not Eddie Kolb."

"Who is it then?" Kopasz asked.

"We don't have a match as of yet," Emory answered. "But the results are 98.9 percent certain that it isn't Kolb."

The room was silent. *Fuck*, Carl thought to himself. No Glenda, no Eddie, just a crazy lady living in their house with a nameless frozen stiff.

"Have you taken fingerprints from the lady at the hospital?" It was Emory. All eyes turned to him.

"Uh, no," Carl offered after clearing his throat.

"We could take a ride out there and get them," Emory said. "And while we're there get a DNA sample."

"Don't you need something to compare it to?" asked the man Carl hadn't recognized. He was in his late thirties and was wearing a decent looking suit and starched white shirt.

"Eventually, yes," Emory answered. "My thought is that we'll have a sample for comparison if we need it at some point."

"Sounds good," Chief Kopasz offered. "Carl since you missed introductions this is Jeff Devry from the state BCI," he said indicating the man who had just asked the question. The Bureau of Criminal Investigation was the state's plain clothes unit. "He'll be on loan to us until we can get this thing cleared up."

Carl nodded at Devry. He tried to get an impression of him, albeit a quick one. Was this guy some hotshot sent to take over the case? He glanced down at Captain D'Agostino, who was looking back at him impassively. He knew D'Agostino was probably taking heat from the Chief and had to admit to himself that they had accomplished next to nothing so far.

"Alright," the Chief's voice brought Carl back to the present. "Here's what we're going to do. Carl, as of now this is your only case. All of your other open cases will be reassigned. I want you to bring Detective Devry up to speed and by that I mean go back to the start. The house on Pinehurst, the canvas, witness statements, everything." He looked down the table at Carl who nodded back. "Nick, are you good with all this?" he asked D'Agostino.

"Yep," D'Agostino answered.

"Okay," Kopasz said rising from his chair. "Let's get to work."

Ten minutes later Carl, Devry, and Emory were in D'Agostino's office. D'Agostino looked agitated, obviously he had taken the meeting with the Chief as a dressing down. Bill Miller knocked on the door jamb and stepped into the room.

"Good," D'Agostino started. "Miller I want you to take inspector Emory out to the County Home and get him whatever he needs in regard to our unknown subject." He turned towards Carl, "Detective Wisniewski," (Carl noticed the captain was no longer on a first name basis with his underlings.) "You heard the Chief. Give Detective Devry access to all your notes and take him to the crime scene when he's ready."

"Still not sure if that's where the murder took place Cap," Carl offered.

D'Agostino glared at him for a moment and then said, "We're not sure of very much are we?"

Point taken, Carl thought. The room was silent for an awkward moment until D'Agostino sat back in his chair and said, "Okay, let's go!"

The four men started to file out of the office and D'Agostino said, "'Hold on Carl." Carl turned around and D'Agostino added, "Shut the door."

Carl could feel his neck get hot again. Here we go, he thought. "What's up?" he asked.

D'Agostino stood up and walked around his desk until he was just a few feet from Carl. He spoke quietly but firmly. "Look me in the eye and tell me you're up to this?"

"What the hell are you talking about?" Carl responded.

"Four weeks and we have no idea whose body turned up in a freezer on a dead end street, who the shut-in was who was living with the body or the location of the people who supposedly live in said house."

Carl shrugged, "It's not like this was an open and shut case."

"No it's not," D'Agostino said, his voice turning into a low growl. "It's obviously going to require some actual work on our part to see it through."

"Captain, with all due respect, what do you think we've been doing? Playing with ourselves?"

D'Agostino stepped closer until he was a foot away from Carl. He furrowed his brow and said, "I don't know what you're doing. Maybe all I see is a guy just punching the clock until he puts his papers in."

"Bullshit," Carl shot back.

"Oh really? Who else would walk into the Chief of Police's office, reeking of booze with nothing to say for the past four weeks?"

Carl was stunned. He wanted to tell D'Agostino to fuck himself right then and there but caught himself. He just glared back at D'Agostino and said nothing. D'Agostino finally broke eye contact and turned back to his desk. "So here we are," the Captain said. "The Chief is pulling in favors from his contacts in the Sheriff's office and the State Police. Unless you get something and get it fast, he's going to turn it over to the State guys." He looked back at Carl as he sat down. "Make something happen Carl, and soon."

Carl walked out of the office, using everything in his power not to slam the door on the way out.

"Carl?" It was Miller.

"What?" Carl growled.

"Hey man, don't bite my head off…"

"Jesus Christ, Miller, what is it?"

Miller handed him a sheet of paper. "Give this guy a call. He lives next door to the Kolb place but he's been out of town visiting relatives for the last month."

Carl looked at the paper. It had a name, address, phone number on it and nothing else.

Miller added, "He said he wanted to talk to the guy in charge. He said he's got a lot to say about the goings on at 127 Pinehurst."

Fourteen

Winter/Spring, 1977

School was closed the entire first week of February as the area dug itself out after the blizzard. Mike's father was working overtime at the rail yard as city crews were loading snow onto hopper cars in an effort to clear the snow clogged streets. When his father was home he was either in the basement or in bed. Mike did notice one difference since he had been cutting his father a wide swath lately. His father had turned his vitriol towards his mother, anything from her cooking to her housekeeping to her appearance. His mother wasn't an unattractive woman. She was petite and dressed modestly. Still his father seemed to go out of his way to disparage her.

Mike seldom saw Mark Collins any more. Basketball season was in full swing and Mark was starting for the freshman team. As long as Mike could remember, Mark could be found shooting baskets in his driveway at the hoop Mark's father had affixed to the side of the Collins' house.

To fill the void, Mike found himself spending more time with Larry Arnetto and his cousin Nick.

Larry's father was a cement contractor and fairly successful. Larry had nice clothes and his older brother and sister had their own cars. Larry's mother was always home though and ruled the house with an iron fist. Nick, on the other hand, lived alone with his father on Meadow Place and his father always seemed to be at work or elsewhere so a lot of time was spent at Nick's. The lower flat Nick and his father lived in was usually untidy and reeked of cigarettes. Still it was better than hanging around out in the cold or under Larry's mother's watchful eye. Even better, Nick's father had bought him a foosball table which the landlady, who lived upstairs, allowed them to keep in the basement.

It was after school on a Tuesday during the first week of March. Mike, Nick and Larry got off the bus at the corner of Genesee and Meadow. The temperature was in the thirties but chest high piles of snow still remained from the blizzard.

"You guys coming over?" Nick asked. He was wearing a denim jacket with a hooded sweatshirt underneath as usual. If he had a winter coat, he was too cool to wear it.

"Can't," Larry answered. "My mom needs me to do something."

Nick smirked at his cousin and then turned to Mike. "How about you? Or do you need to run home to Mommy too?"

"Screw you Nick," Larry said and turned to leave.

"Sure," Mike said. He turned to head down Meadow Place towards Nick's house when Nick grabbed his sleeve.

"Hang on," Nick said. "I need to go to Tops and get some smokes."

Mike looked at Nick. He was serious. "Okay," he shrugged.

Tops Supermarket was on Genesee Street, a few hundred feet from the bus stop. Mike had his Social Studies book with a few papers crammed inside it. Nick, as usual, had nothing. They walked down the street and across the parking lot.

Mike knew there was a cigarette vending machine at the front of the store. He had seen it himself when his mother had sent him for milk or bread in the past. He had been sneaking the occasional cigarette from his dad's pack of menthols when the old man was asleep but had never bought his own. He followed Nick, who strolled casually into the store as he fished some change out of his jean's pocket. Mike looked around the front of the store. There were a few open registers with cashiers checking people out but little other activity. He heard Nick deposit his money and pull the lever. He looked towards the machine as Nick was retrieving the pack from the tray at the bottom. There was a sticker on the top right hand corner of the machine that said; *New York State law prohibits the sale of tobacco products to any individual under the age of 18* in red letters.

"Let's go," Nick said. They walked towards the front entrance and then heard a voice behind them.

"Hey!"

Mike turned around to look for the source and saw a large man in a shirt and tie walking towards them. He was in his forties and his stomach was hanging over his belt.

"Keep walking," Nick said quietly.

"Hey!" The man repeated, louder this time. Nick had already walked out the front door but Mike had frozen for just a moment. When he did turn to leave, the man, who was deceptively quick for his size, caught up to him and grabbed him by his coat collar just as he crossed the threshold. Mike looked to Nick who looked like he was on the verge of taking off.

"What do you think you're doing?" the man asked, tightening his grip on Mike's collar.

"Let him go," Nick said defiantly.

"What's the matter with you two? Can't you read?"

A low rumble grew louder. Eddie Kolb's Dodge pulled up to the front of the store where the three were standing. He switched off the car and climbed out. "Is there a problem? he asked.

"Just a couple of juveniles breaking the law, if it's all the same to you," the store manager said.

Mark knew that Eddie had been home for a few weeks. He heard the Dodge rumbling down the street from time to time and once when he was walking home, Eddie had passed him and he could have sworn that Eddie had nodded at him. Now Eddie smiled, the corners of his Fu-Manchu mustache turning up. Even from a distance of twenty feet, Eddie was an imposing figure. He stood six foot four and his broad shoulders filled out the army jacket he was wearing.

"I'm sorry, has my nephew done something wrong?" he asked, indicating Mike.

"Your nephew?" the manager replied looking down at Mike. "Yeah, he and his underage pal here were buying cigarettes."

Eddie didn't miss a beat, "Oh shit, that's my fault. Those were for me. I sent them in while I ran an errand." Eddie walked around the front of the car and held out his hand to Nick. Nick hesitated momentarily and then quickly handed the cigarettes to Eddie.

The manager didn't reply at first, but Mike could feel his grip loosening.

"I really am sorry," Eddie added.

"Next time," the manager replied, letting go of Mike's collar, "please don't send a minor to buy them."

"Understood," Eddie said, walking back to the driver's side and opening the door. He looked at Mike and added, "Okay, hop in boys."

Mike quickly went to the passenger side door and lifted the seat to let himself in back. Nick was waiting to climb into the front seat when he turned to the store manager, who was still standing there.

"To answer your question, yeah, I can read," Nick said. "Can you read this?" he asked, raising his middle finger.

Mike saw the store manager frown and then, Eddie's long arm

reach across the passenger seat, grab Nick by the belt and yanked him into the car.

"Ow! Jesus, take it easy," Nick protested as he shut the door.

"You've got to learn to cut your losses, little man."

Nick shot a look at Eddie but looked away when he saw Eddie's expression. The smile was gone and he looked mean, scary mean. Eddie put the car in gear and pulled away from the front of the store. He turned left on Genesee and caught Mike's eye in the rearview mirror.

"Been meaning to talk to you," Eddie said.

Mike tried to respond, but nothing came out. Fortunately, Eddie had broken eye contact and was focused on the turn onto Meadow.

"My old lady told me what you did for her during the storm," Eddie continued. "Thanks."

Again, Mike had no words, he just nodded. "You seem like a smart kid," Eddie offered. Mike noticed that they had passed Nick's apartment and were headed towards Clover Place.

"I'm not too sure about your friend here," Eddie went on, nodding at Nick. "But you seem like a good kid." Mike saw Nick look sideways at Eddie. "Why don't you guys stop at the house? I've got something for you."

A few minutes later, Mike and Nick were following Eddie Kolb through the kitchen door at the back of the house. Mike thought Eddie must have been home for at least two or three weeks but nothing seemed to have changed. There were still dishes in the sink and the kitchen garbage can was on the verge of overflowing. Eddie pulled his work boots off and left them on a mat by the door. The boys did the same. Glenda was nowhere in sight but there was music coming from the living room. Eddie fished the cigarettes out of his coat pocket and tossed them to Nick. "You guys have a seat," he said. "I'll be right back." He left the room and they heard him climb the stairs.

Nick went to open the cigarettes and Mike shook his head. Nick snorted and pointed to the ashtray at the center of the table. "Don't be a fag," Nick said. He pulled a lighter from his jeans pocket and was just about to light up when Eddie came back into the kitchen.

"Hold on there, little hero," Eddie said. He was carrying a small tin box. He sat down across from Nick and looked at him. "I wanted to thank your friend here for what he did for Glenda," he said shifting his gaze towards Mike. He pulled the top off the box and pulled out a plastic bag.

Nick looked at Mike with a questioning look. Of course Mike hadn't told anyone about sneaking into the Kolb's house during the blizzard and finding Glenda almost catatonic. Mike could smell the weed as soon as Eddie opened the bag. He knew what it was. One of the restrooms at in the 11-12 building at school where the juniors and seniors had most of their classes reeked of it on occasion, but this was as close as he'd ever been.

Nick was trying to look cool but Mike could tell he was as nervous as he was. They watched Eddie take a pack of rolling papers from the tin and skillfully roll a joint. He put the joint in his mouth, took a Zippo lighter from his flannel shirt pocket and brought it up to light it.

"Look at you two," Eddie laughed. "A couple of hoodlums like yourselves? You're telling me you never got high before?"

Mike just shook his head and Nick sat motionless, not wanting to admit it and not wanting to get caught in a lie.

"Jesus, you look like your about to shit your pants," Eddie said as he flicked the lighter. "Okay, my little virgins. The trick is to go slow your first time."

They had both gagged with the first hit, to Eddie's amusement. At first Mike didn't feel any different, but then he felt light-headed and slightly disoriented. Then a mix of euphoria and paranoia, mostly the thought that he had no control over his body. He was aware of Eddie talking about Vietnam, the cops and other things. He had lost track of how long he'd been sitting there when Glenda entered the room. She glanced at him seemingly without recognition. Her hair was a mess and her face was creased from sleep. She went to the refrigerator, got a can of beer out and then left the kitchen without a word.

"Alright," Eddie's voice cut through the haze. "I gotta get to work, so you little fuckers need to leave." He was smiling, but there was no warmth behind his smile.

Mike and Nick unsteadily pulled on their shoes and left through the back door. "You guys ever need anything," Eddie said from behind them, "you know where I am."

They walked around for a while until Mike felt like his head had cleared enough for him to go home. That night, during a typically quiet dinner, he sensed that his father was looking at him, but he kept his head down, finished eating and went up to his room without incident.

FIFTEEN

JUNE 20, 1988

Carl was still fuming by the time he and Jeff Devry were making their way down Union

Road in the unmarked Ford towards the Kolb residence. Thankfully, Devry had the case folder open on his lap and was pouring through the first few pages. Carl was in no mood for small talk. Finally, as Carl turned left onto Clover Place, Devry broke the silence.

"I want you to know I'm not here to step on your toes and take over the investigation," he said.

Carl nodded. He was still too angry to be polite.

"I'm here at the request of your Chief, just an extra set of eyes."

"You do a lot of homicides?" Carl managed.

"A few. I'm based here in Buffalo and mostly do investigations for the State court. But I've caught a few."

Carl nodded again. His anger was slowly ebbing and he didn't want to take it out on Devry.

"We have a fresh witness to interview," he offered. "After that I'll give you a tour of the Kolb place."

"Sounds good."

A few minutes later, they pulled up in front of the Kolb house and climbed out of the car. It still had yet to rain that month but the air was heavy and humid. Carl looked at the sheet Miller had given him at the station. He pointed at the house to the right of the

Kolb's. "Stanley Lewandowski, 110 Pinehurst," he said.

"He was out of town when the body was discovered?" Devry asked.

"Yeah, visiting a sister in Orlando."

They walked up the front walk to Lewandowski's home. It was a small, one story house with vinyl siding and a neatly trimmed lawn. It looked like a palace compared to the Kolb house next door.

Carl rang the bell and waited. A moment later the door opened and a short, pudgy man in his sixties opened the door. He looked at Carl and then Devry as his eyes adjusted to the daylight.

"Yes?"

"Mr. Lewandowski, I'm Detective Wisniewski and this is Detective Devry from the State Police. I understand you wanted to talk to us about your neighbors, the Kolbs."

Just then a small white dog with rheumy eyes limped up to the door, yipping like crazy. Lewandowski said something in Polish and pushed the dog back into the house with his foot. He stepped out onto the stoop, almost bumping into Carl and shut the door. Beads of perspiration had formed on his bald scalp. Carl and Devry had to step off the stoop to make room. Lewandowski turned and looked at them with a frown on his face. "You're about fifteen years too late," he said.

One of *those* guys, Carl thought to himself. "What do you mean?" he asked.

Lewandowski pointed at the Kolb House, "Those people," he spat. "I lost count of the times I called about the parties, the music, the cars..."

Carl held his hands up. "Mr. Lewandowski..."

"And I know they were selling drugs!" Lewandowski went on.

"Forty years I lived here. This was a nice neighborhood. But then this trash moves in and it goes to Hell, no thanks to you guys!"

"Are you done?" Carl asked flatly.

"Excuse me?" Lewandowski raised his eyebrows. Clearly he was expecting a different response to his rant.

"Sir," Devry cut in. "We're investigating a possible homicide that may have taken place at your neighbor's house."

Lewandowski broke his stare away from Carl and looked at Devry slightly confused. He opened his mouth to say something but Devry stared back at him and went on, "While we're sorry to hear that you may have been inconvenienced by…"

"Inconvenienced?" Lewandowski sputtered.

Devry pressed on, raising his voice slightly while adding some grit to it. "Inconvenienced by your neighbors. What's done is done and we have an investigation to conduct."

Lewandowski's face turned red and he was shaking his head. Devry took a step closer to him. Even though Lewandowski was on the stoop they were nearly eye to eye. Devry lowered his voice and said, "Now we can either stand here sweating our balls off and yelling at each other or you can answer Detective Wisniewski's questions and we'll be on our way."

That seemed to take the steam out of Lewandowski. His shoulders drooped and he looked back at Carl. "What do you want to know?" he asked.

Carl was grateful. He had been considering giving the old guy a slap with the mood he was in but now Devry had made him compliant.

Carl took out his notebook and pen. "Do you know who was living in the house besides Glenda Kolb?"

Lewandowski rubbed the stubble on his chin and considered for a moment. "You mean the old lady? Never talked to the old bat," he began. "My wife Dorothy, she used to try to talk to the younger one…"

"Glenda Kolb?" Carl prompted.

"I guess," Lewandowski shrugged. "Weird little girl. But Dorothy went out of her way to be nice to her, said she seemed sad and lonely. One of the few conversations she had with her, the girl said the lady was her aunt."

"When did this lady move in with Glenda?" Carl asked.

"A couple of years ago, I think."

"And you never spoke to her?"

"Never," Lewandowski shook his head. "Only caught sight of her a few times through the window. I can't remember seeing her outside the house except for a few times. And the younger one… Glenda? She was about as friendly as a rabid skunk. After my Dorothy passed last year…" Lewandowski's voice trailed off as he seemed to be lost in thought.

"And Glenda Kolb?" Carl pressed on. "When was the last time you saw her?"

The old man shook his head. "Don't honestly remember."

"And Eddie Kolb?"

Lewandowski frowned at the mention of Eddie. "That punk! It's been a long time and I can't say I miss him."

"You mentioned he may have been dealing drugs?" Devry asked.

"I know he was! Cars coming and going at all hours. Coons, Spics and all kinds of white trash."

Carl thought Lewandowski's vitriol was getting them off track and he had to get him back on it. "Anybody you recognize come by the house?" he asked.

Lewandowski looked at Carl for a moment and then said. "Just a few of the neighborhood street rats. Couldn't tell you any names." He looked down at his feet for a moment and then added. "Oh yeah, once in a while the old guy from around the corner would come by during the day. I don't know what he was doing with those people…"

"What old guy?" Carl prompted.

"I dunno…" Lewandowski shrugged somewhat exasperated. "Lives on the corner of Clover and Woodbine. Big guy. I thought he was a retired cop or something. Don't you know him?" Carl felt a bead of sweat run down his back. Lewandowski had just described Bob Czerczak, who had failed to mention that he'd been to the Kolb house. *What the fuck Bob?* He thought to himself. He was making notes but he could see Devry shift his weight and look at him.

"Yeah," Carl said looking back up at Lewandowski. "I know who that is and we've already spoken to him." He took a card out of his jacket pocket and handed it to Lewandowski. "Thank you Mr. Lewandowski. If we need anything else we'll be in contact. In the meantime, if you think of anything that we may have missed please call the detective bureau at this number."

Lewandowski squinted at the card and frowned again. "Yeah, sure," he said somewhat peevishly. Carl and Devry turned to make their way down the drive when Lewandowski spoke,

"The aunt…"

Carl and Devry turned around. "What about her?" Devry asked before Carl could.

"Dorothy said she was from around here. She said she'd seen her before at mass at Our Lady Help of Christians and at bingo a couple of times with her kid."

Carl looked at Devry who just nodded and said, "Thank you again, Mr. Lewandowski."

Sixteen
Spring 1977

THE SCHOOL YEAR was drawing to a close. Mike had maintained decent grades with what he considered minimal effort. In his meeting with his guidance counselor for next year he was steered towards shop classes. Not that he objected, he preferred to work with his hands. Nick, on the other hand, had barely passed freshman year and had been suspended twice, once for fighting and another time for smoking in the boy's room. He only saw Mark Collins on the bus now. They were cordial but he knew something had changed.

One Friday night in June, his mother was at Bingo and his father was working a double shift. He was hanging out at Larry's house with Larry and Nick playing bumper pool in the basement.

"We should go do something," Nick said.

"Like what?" Mike asked.

Larry took his shot and then looked at the clock on the basement wall. "It's almost nine o'clock, I can't go out now."

Nick laughed. "Is it bedtime already?"

"Screw you Nicky," Larry shot back.

"Watch that language young man!" Nick laughed again.

"What did you have in mind?" Mike asked. He had to admit to himself he was bored. Larry's parents were upstairs and the door was open. The mood in the basement was somewhat stifled.

"We could go see your girlfriend on Pinehurst," Nick said with a smirk.

Mike felt his face flush. Nick had come up with the idea that Mike was smitten with Glenda Kolb and teased Mike about it whenever he had the chance.

"Or at least her old man," Nick continued.

"And do what?" Larry asked.

Nick stared at his cousin. They had told Larry about their encounter with Eddie Kolb as Larry listened in amazement.

On the surface, the idea terrified Mike. There was something about Eddie Kolb that was truly unsettling. But he was restless and bored. It was almost summer break and although he was grateful to be out of school, the idea of spending the summer under his father's thumb depressed him. He needed to do something, even if it was risky.

Larry was shaking his head, "I can't," he said in a near whisper. "My dad will ask where I'm going and..."

"Tell him you're going to my house," Nick interrupted.

Larry just continued to shake his head.

Nick went on, "What about you Schultz? You going to be a pussy too?"

"Let's go," Mike replied.

They left Larry mumbling to himself and headed out into the cool night air. Ten minutes later they were on Pinehurst, standing in front of the Kolb's house. There were two other cars in the driveway behind Eddie's. All the lights were on and the faint sound of music was coming out of the house. Mike looked at Nick who seemed to have lost some of his bravado. "Well?" He asked. Nick nodded and headed up the driveway towards the back of the house.

They stood just short of the concrete step that led to the back door. The curtains were drawn and they could hear voices over the sound of a Lynyrd Skynyrd record playing on the Hi-fi. Once again, Nick seemed unusually unsure of himself. Mike stepped up onto the stoop and knocked loudly on the door. Nothing happened for a moment. Mike thought about retreating but then he saw a silhouette enter the kitchen and come to the door. The curtain was drawn aside and Glenda peered out into the darkness. She frowned and opened the door and looked out. It took her eyes a moment to adjust but she recognized Mike and smiled.

"Hey," she said. "What are you doing here?" She was obviously buzzed but her smile was genuine and disarming.

Mike was dumbstruck. He tried to speak but all that came out was, "Um..."

She looked past Mike at Nick. "Who's your friend?" Nick also was unable to offer a response.

She obviously had no recollection that Nick had been in her home before.

Mike finally found the nerve to speak. "That's Nick. Eddie said we should stop by if..." here, Mike hesitated again.

"If what?" Glenda looked at him teasingly.

"Who is it, babe?" Eddie's voice came from behind Glenda. He had entered the kitchen with a beer in one hand and a cigarette in the other. Glenda stood aside and Eddie looked out at the boys and laughed.

"Oh shit!" he roared. "It's my nephew and his delinquent buddy. Get in here you two!"

Glenda looked at Eddie quizzically and then stepped aside further to let the boys enter.

The music was loud and the house smelled of cigarettes and

weed. Glenda closed the door behind them and Eddie said, "You youngsters care for a brew?"

"Sure," Nick said before Mike could answer.

"Hook these two hooligans up, babe," Eddie said to Glenda.

Glenda looked at Eddie disapprovingly but went to the refrigerator and brought out two bottles of Genesee and handed them to Mike and Nick. "Come into the parlor boys," Eddie said and turned around to leave the kitchen. Mike glanced back at Glenda who had gone to the counter to refill her glass with vodka. He followed Nick and Eddie into the living room.

The song "Sweet Home Alabama" was in its dying strains on the record player. "What the fuck?" came a voice from the couch. It was a slight man in his twenties with lank blond hair and a mustache. He was looking at Mike and Nick incredulously. "Who the fuck invited the boy scouts?"

"Can it, Spider," Eddie said to the man. "This is Mike and his buddy..." Eddie looked at Nick.

"Nick," Nick said.

"Yeah, Nick," Eddie said snapping his fingers.

Glenda had entered the room, glass in hand and took a seat in the beat up recliner. There was another man in the room, seated in a kitchen chair that had been pulled into the living room. He was heavy set with dark hair, dark deep set eyes and a bushy beard.

Another song started to play and Eddie plopped down on the couch next to Spider. He spoke up, "Boys, this is Spider and that hulking mass over there is Tony," he said pointing to the other man. Mike noticed that there was nowhere else to sit so he took a pull off the skunky beer and struck what he thought was a casual pose.

"So," Eddie said, "What brings you two to our humble home?"

Mike shuffled his feet and thought about how to broach the subject. Nick wasn't reluctant anymore. "We were wondering if we could buy some pot," he said.

Spider laughed and passed beer through his nose. He wiped his face with the sleeve of his worn leather jacket and said, "Jesus Christ, do you even have hair on your nuts yet?"

Mike could feel himself blush. He was starting to think that this was a mistake.

"Ask your mom," he heard Nick say.

It took a second but the smile disappeared from Spider's face. The only sound in the room was coming from the record player. Suddenly Eddie burst out laughing. "Holy shit," he said. "The kid has balls, even if they are hairless."

Mike could still feel the tension in the air. He glanced at Nick, whose face had turned red also but was staring at Spider who was staring back at him with malice. He glanced at Glenda who seemed to have zoned out and couldn't care less about what was happening.

"Tell you what," Eddie said. "You two go have a seat in the kitchen and I'll check my inventory."

Mike and Nick retreated to the kitchen and sat at the table. "Are you nuts?" Mike asked Nick just loudly enough to be heard above the music.

Nick still looked genuinely angry. It took a moment for the question to sink in and then he answered, "Fuck that asshole," he said loudly. Mike put a hand on Nick's arm just as Eddie came into the kitchen with a rectangular tin box. He pulled out a chair and sat down next to Mike.

"You're in luck boys," he said. He removed the cover from the box and pulled out a baggie with about a half inch of marijuana in the bottom. "I'm assuming you two aren't in the market for a large amount, so I thought you might be interested in a nickel bag."

Mike nodded and looked at Nick. "Sure," Nick said.

"For you two," Eddie said looking at them, "Let's say twenty-five bucks."

Mike was dumbstruck again. He realized that he had not asked Nick how he had intended to pay for it. He himself had three dollars in his pocket.

"I've got ten bucks on me," Nick offered.

"Hmm, how about you?" Eddie looked at Mike.

"Three."

Eddie let out an exaggerated sigh. "Boys," he said. "I'm not running a charity here. This isn't the skunk weed that you could buy off some spade on Jefferson Street."

The boys sat silently while Eddie looked from one to the other. "And I'm not in the habit of fronting bags to first time buyers. It's bad business." He put the bag back in the tin box, sat back and folded his arms across his chest. "I'll tell you what. I'll sell you the bag for thirteen if you two consider doing me favors now and then."

"What kind of favors?" Nick asked.

"You two go to school at Maryvale right?"

They both nodded.

"Well, I guess it's not so much a favor as it is an opportunity," he said taking the bag back out. Mike and Nick were both sitting up now, hanging on Eddie's every word.

"I lost my guy at the school and it's such a fertile market. I imagine a couple of bright young lads, such as yourselves, could discreetly become my new salesmen at school in the fall." He looked at them again and pushed the bag into the center of the table.

Mike felt his stomach tying itself in a knot. He wanted to turn Eddie's offer down or at least say he'd think about it and get the Hell out of the house. Nick, of course, had other ideas.

"Sure," he said. He stood up and pulled a ten dollar bill out of his jeans. He looked at Mike and nodded. "We're in."

Mike stood up and took out his three wrinkled one dollar bills. *What the hell?* He thought. He'd come this far with Nick and now there was no turning back. His apprehension was ebbing suddenly for reasons he couldn't fathom.

Eddie laughed and stood up. He fished a pack of rolling papers out of his shirt pocket and handed them to Mike. "I'll throw these in. I'm sure you'll need them." He looked at the kitchen clock and added. "Getting late. You two should be on your way. Stop by in a couple of weeks and we can hash things out."

Without another word, Mike and Nick stood up, went to the door and back out into the cool night air. "Let's go up the hill," Nick said, gesturing towards the stairs at the end of the street that went up the side of the Genesee Street overpass.

Mike's mind was racing. Not only had he bought his first bag of pot but now he had tentatively agreed to work for Eddie Kolb. He followed Nick up the steps in silence. Nick, for his part, seemed lost in thought himself. A few minutes later they were behind the Volkswagen dealership and Nick was clumsily trying to roll a joint.

"You sure know how to make an impression," Mike said.

"What are you talking about?" Nick asked twisting the ends of the joint.

"That guy, Spider, was pretty pissed about that 'your mom' crack."

Nick examined his handiwork as he fished a lighter out of his jacket pocket. "Fuck him," he said.

"I don't know. It looked like he wanted to kick your ass."

A breeze kicked up and Nick struggled with the lighter. "Help me out here," he said. Mike put his hands up to help block the wind and Nick finally lit the end of the joint and took a drag. A seed popped and the paper was burning unevenly but he managed to take a long pull without coughing. He passed the joint to Mike and exhaled. He looked off into the distance and said, "That guy's a piece of shit. You can't let somebody like that run you down."

Mike took a drag and fought off the urge to cough. He looked at Nick whose face was dimly illuminated by a distant street light. He exhaled and asked, "So what if he came after you and Eddie decides he's not going to get in his way?"

"What do you mean?"

"What would you do?"

Nick took the joint back and said, "Whatever I had to."

Mike considered what that might mean. Nick wasn't particularly physically imposing but he carried himself like he was unafraid of most anything.

"Did I ever tell you why my parents split up?" Nick asked.

"No."

"My older brother, he's pretty fucked up. Like a real mental case. He's been in hospitals and on medication since he was little. One doctor said he was schizophrenic. Anyway he used to kick the shit out of me until one day last year when he was starting his shit and I pushed him down a flight of stairs. My mom, she's freaking out and saying that 'he can't help it, he's sick.' And she's screaming at me asking me how I could do that. And my dad he's like, "We should put him in the nuthouse before he hurts somebody.""

"Shit," Mike said.

"Yeah," Nick said after exhaling again. "It was pretty cut and dried after that. My mom was going to do everything she could to keep my brother from being put away and my old man wanted no part of it."

Mike took the joint back and said nothing. Nick looked at him and said, "You gotta stand up for yourself or you're gonna be taking beatings the rest of your life."

Seventeen

Carl took his pocket knife and cut the crime scene tape on the Kolb's front door. He folded the knife and unlocked the padlock that had been installed to dissuade any curious locals from having a look inside the house. At his recommendation, both he and Devry had removed their suit jackets and put them in the car. Devry had pulled a pair of latex gloves from his pocket. He looked over the roof at Carl and offered him a pair.

"The lab guys from the state and county have already been through here with a fine-toothed comb," Carl said. "I doubt they'll be back."

"Well, maybe to protect you from the crime scene? If it's as bad as you say." Devry offered.

"Good point."

As soon as Carl pushed the door open they were hit by a blast of hot, fetid air and the smell of decay. It was worse than he imagined. The house had been closed up for weeks, and since it was still considered a potential crime scene, no one had been allowed to enter it to clean or remove anything. "First stop, the basement," Carl said, flicking on his flashlight. The two men went through the kitchen and down into the basement. If anything the passing of time and the lack of ventilation had made the smell worse in the basement. Carl fought off the urge to gag as he led Devry into the room where the body was found.

"Shit," Devry said. Carl noticed that Devry had covered his mouth and nose with a handkerchief.

"Yeah," Carl coughed. He stepped back to let Devry take a quick look into the freezer and then around the rest of the room. He wondered if Devry thought he was going to see anything that two lab crews had missed and crack the case.

"Let's get the fuck out of here," Devry said suddenly. They went back upstairs into the living room. Devry looked around the kitchen. Carl noticed he wasn't touching anything, just looking around and thinking to himself.

Carl was wondering how long Devry was going to make him stand around in the heat and the stench when Devry casually asked a question. "So who's this ex-cop the neighbor was talking about?"

Shit, Carl thought. He wasn't ready for this. He had to stall. "If it's who I think it is, there was a name in the canvas report."

Devry looked at him. "And who is that? You said you knew him?"

Carl could feel the beads of perspiration beading on his forehead. "Mostly by reputation. Guy named Bob Czerczak. He retired in the seventies."

Devry considered that for a moment and then asked, "What kind of reputation are we talking about?"

Carl shook his head. He was giving Devry the wrong idea. "Nothing like that. The guy was a local legend, that's what I meant."

Devry nodded and went past Carl into the living room.

Carl continued, "Old school cop, nice to the old ladies and kids, but if you were doing something hinky he wouldn't hesitate to crack your skull."

Devry stepped over to the open front door and took a deep breath. He smiled and said, "Yeah, sounds like my old man. Did he mention that he knew the Kolbs when he was interviewed?"

Carl shook his head. "I don't think he did. I'd have to check the file."

"Let's go take a look," Devry said and then walked out the front door.

After Carl had rescued the padlock the two men were sitting in the unmarked car. Carl had turned the air conditioner on full and it was finally starting to have an effect. He could feel the perspiration had soaked through his t-shirt and into his dress shirt. Devry was leafing through the file on his lap.

"Here he is," Devry said. "Robert Czerczak, still lives in the neighborhood." He looked over at Carl. "Nothing here mentions that he knew the Kolbs. Want to go have a word with Mr. Czerczak?"

"Why not?" Carl responded, trying to hide his unease.

A minute later they had parked in Bob Czerczak's driveway and were approaching the front door. Carl involuntarily hesitated. Devry looked at him and then motioned to the front door. "You want to do the honors?" Devry asked. "It might be better coming from a local guy." Carl nodded and walked up to the front door silently hoping that Czerczak was at physical therapy or anywhere else besides at home. This was a conversation he didn't want to have in front of Devry. Carl rang the bell and stood back. The seconds ticked by and nothing happened.

"I'll check the garage," he heard Devry say from behind him. Out of his peripheral Carl saw one of the front curtains move. He looked over and made eye contact with Czerczak who was peeking out from behind the curtain. Carl shook his head at Czerczak. A second later the curtain was closed. Carl went through the motions of knocking on the door.

He looked at Devry who was peering through one of the small windows in the door to the attached garage. "There's a car in there," he said. "Doesn't look like it's been driven lately. There's about a half an inch of dust on the roof."

Carl nodded. "We can try to call him or stop back later," he said.

"Sounds good," Devry said.

As they climbed back into the unmarked Ford, Carl's head started pounding again. Probably a combination of the hangover and his ire at Bob Czerczak. Why had Big Bob lied to him about not knowing the Kolb's? He glanced over at Devry who was paging through the file again. He hoped he'd have time to figure this all out.

Eighteen

October 1977

It was a month and a half into the school year. Things at Mike's house had gotten worse. The railroad that his father worked for had been in bankruptcy and was being absorbed by a new company. With expenses and payroll being cut, his father was working fewer hours and spending more time at home, most of it spent drinking in the basement. His mother had become withdrawn, barely speaking to anyone. Mike avoided being home like the plague. School offered some respite. Once again, he was getting by in his courses, excelling even in wood shop and electric shop. He enjoyed working with his hands and found the concentration it involved a welcome distraction.

Nick seemed to be on the school's radar. He had been summoned to Mr. Baker's office more than a few times for skipping classes and on one occasion, he was grilled after someone vandalized one of the restrooms. He was either failing or close to failing all of his classes.

Eddie had started them off slowly in the business with a stern warning about being discreet. He would meet them in the parking lot of the donut shop down the street from school with a few nickel bags. They could keep five dollars for every bag they sold.

It was a Friday night in mid-October and they were holding a few bags. Mike told his mother he was going to hang out at Nick's and met Nick at the fire hall at the end of Clover Place. There was a chill in the air and a light mist was falling. They crossed Union Road and headed west on Southcrest.

"Who is this kid again?" Mike asked.

"Marty Coyle," Nick answered. "He's having a party. He's bought from me before. Trust me, he'll be happy to see us."

Fifteen minutes later they were walking down Diane Drive and knew they were approaching the house almost immediately. There were cars in front of the house and in the drive. A few kids were standing outside the side door smoking. Coyle's parents must be out of town or extremely lenient, Mike thought to himself. Mike hesitated briefly but Nick was already halfway up the driveway so he double-timed it to catch up. As they were about to enter two girls came bursting through the side door. The first girl barely made it outside when she threw up all over the side of a car parked just outside the door. Mike recognized the second girl, Kim, from school. Kim reached over her sick friend and tried to pull her hair back as she continued to retch on the side of the car. Mike felt a tug on his sleeve and looked up to see Nick urging him into the house.

They walked into the kitchen and there were a few kids standing around engaged in conversation. There were plastic cups all over the counter and the place smelled of spilled beer and cigarettes. The sound of a Styx song was coming from the basement. Nick went down the stairs with Mike right behind him.

The paneled basement was dimly lit and the music was loud. As Mike's vision adjusted to the gloom he saw that the room was packed. A tall, heavy-set kid, wearing a varsity jacket barged past them and made his way up the stairs.

"Fucking jock," Nick said loud enough for the tall kid to hear him. The kid turned around and gave Nick a dirty look and then made his way up the stairs.

Mike was already uncomfortable. The room was stuffy and it was full of upperclassmen as far as he could tell. "Where's your buddy?" he shouted into Nick's ear.

Nick just shrugged and made his way into the crowd. Mike followed him and halfway across the room, Nick stopped in front of a pimply faced kid with sandy brown hair wearing a light blue crew neck sweater.

"What's up, Marty?" Nick yelled above the din.

Marty Coyle looked at Nick with glassy eyes. It took him a moment but then a look of recognition. "What are you doing here?" he asked.

Mike was even more anxious now. Nick had led him to believe that he had been invited. Coyle's demeanor said otherwise.

Nick was undeterred. "Heard you were having a party," he said. "Just wondered if you need anything?"

Coyle stared at Nick without comprehension, he was obviously drunk, stoned or both. Finally he shook his head and said, "Nah, nothing from you man. Especially if you're still selling that same skunk weed you sold me."

Nick laughed. "Skunk weed? That was good stuff I sold you."

Mike was shoved roughly aside. The kid with the varsity jacket had returned to the basement and was now tapping Nick on the shoulder. Nick turned around with anger in his eyes. The kid had at least six inches and forty pounds on Nick.

The name "Wayne" was embroidered on one side of the jacket and an image of a football player in front of a capital M was on the other.

"What?" Nick asked.

Wayne looked at Coyle and asked, "Is this guy a friend of yours, Marty?"

Coyle shook his head. "Just some burnout from school," he answered. "Trying to sell some shitty weed."

"I think you got the wrong party, dirtbag," Wayne said to Nick.

Suddenly, there were two other guys in varsity jackets standing next to them. Nick glared up at Wayne. Mike tried to step in between them but Wayne shoved him aside.

Wayne took a step closer and said, "You got something to say, you little faggot?"

Mike reached around Wayne and grabbed Nick by the sleeve of his denim jacket. "Let's go," he implored.

"Fuck you, mother fucker." Nick said.

Wayne went to grab Nick, but Nick's fist lashed out and caught Wayne's jaw. Wayne was briefly stunned but regained his composure and bull-rushed Nick, grabbing him by the front of his denim jacket. Nick used the larger boy's momentum and spun him around into the stereo cabinet, sending it crashing into the wall. The needle scratched across the record and the music stopped.

"Fuck!" Marty Coyle shouted.

Wayne regained his balance and swung at Nick, the blow glancing off the top of his head as he tried to duck. Wayne grabbed Nick by the collar of his jacket and pulled him into a headlock.

Mike went to help Nick but was grabbed from behind by a pair of strong arms and pulled backwards.

"Fuck," Coyle yelled again looking at the damaged record player. He turned around and looked at Wayne and the struggling Nick and added, "Get them out of here!" Mike would have gone peacefully but he found himself being dragged towards the stairs by two sets of hands now. He could hear Nick swearing and struggling behind him. A girl screamed and Mike heard the sound of a bottle break. He was dragged out the side door of the house and turned around in time to see Nick, still under the control of Wayne and another boy, kick out the glass of the storm door as he was pulled through the door. They were led to the end of the driveway and pushed out into the street.

Nick wasn't finished. He looked back at Wayne with rage in his eyes. "Fuck your mother!"

Wayne laughed and so did the three other members of the football team that had ejected them. This only seemed to further incense Nick. He raised his fists and stepped towards Wayne. Wayne raised his fists also and the two squared off. Wayne feinted with his lead hand a few times and then Nick hit him with a left jab to his eye. If Wayne felt any effect he didn't show it. Nick swung his right hand and Wayne blocked it and grabbed Nick by the arm, pulling him in and then flipping him over onto the wet pavement with a thud. Before Nick could move, Wayne was on top of him, pinning him to the ground with his knees and raining down both fists on Nick's head. Nick tried to cover up but the punches were starting to land.

"Jesus Christ, Porzio!" a voice called out. Wayne stopped punching at the sound of what must have been his last name. He was still looking down at Nick, red faced and angry.

Mike turned towards the sound of the voice. It was Greg Collins, his friend Mark's brother, a senior and also a member of the football team. "You beating up little kids now?" Greg added.

"This fucking burnout broke Coyle's stereo." Wayne grunted.

Nick mumbled something incomprehensible. There was blood coming from his mouth.

Wayne cocked his fist and Greg stepped closer. "I think he's had enough," he said loudly.

Wayne grunted and stood up, giving Nick one last shove into the ground. Nick rolled over and spat blood out onto the pavement.

Greg looked at Mike and shook his head. "Jesus Christ, Schultz. You need to find a better class of friends," he said.

Mike watched as the five upperclassmen and a few spectators moved back towards the house.

He was shaking and felt ashamed that he had just witnessed his friend take a beating without helping at all. He was angry too. It wasn't a fair fight at all. He rushed over to Nick and helped him sit up.

"Fuckin' jocks," Nick swore as he spat out more blood.

Fifteen minutes later they were standing outside a convenience store on the corner of Dick Road and Lydia Lane. Nick was disoriented and was only speaking in sentence fragments. He was a sight. His mouth was still bleeding and his left eye was already starting to swell shut. There was also blood coming from the back of his scalp, probably where Wayne Porzio had bounced it off the pavement. His jacket was wet, dirty and the collar was ripped. There was no way he was going to walk all the way home. A police car drove by on Dick Road and Mike tried to strike a casual pose, hoping they wouldn't see what a bloody mess Nick was. They were still carrying several bags of weed. The cops passed without slowing, but he knew he had to do something. He called the only person he knew he could.

Ten minutes later Eddie Kolb pulled up in the Charger. Mike guided Nick over to the car and helped him into the back seat.

"Holy shit," Eddie said through a plume of cigarette smoke. "Who danced on your friend's face?"

Mike climbed in the front seat and answered, "Some asshole jock at a party."

The tires on the Charger chirped as Eddie pulled out of the parking lot. "They take your stash?" he asked.

It took a moment for Mike to process the question. He shook his head and said, "No."

Eddie chuckled and said, "At least you didn't fuck that up."

"Fuck that!" Nick said from the back seat. Mike looked back at Nick. He had regained consciousness but still looked bleary-eyed and disoriented.

"We need to go back there!" Nick added.

Eddie laughed again and looked at Nick in the rearview mirror. "Not tonight, little hero.

We'll chalk this up as a lesson learned. Starting soon though, we're going to put you runts into my specialized training program so you're not getting your asses kicked on a regular basis."

Mike, looking straight ahead, felt his face flush. He heard Nick mumble something and then he too fell silent.

Nineteen

June 20, 1988

They had been back at the station for a few hours. Carl had gotten a couple of aspirin from one of the dispatchers and the pain in his head had been reduced to a dull throb. He was at a loss. It seemed like the whole situation was slipping out of his grasp. For the first time in a while he had started to worry about his legacy. Was this how he was going to go out? A boozy, washed up dinosaur, shuffling files until it was time to put in his papers?

He was sitting at his desk, paging through the case file again without really reading or comprehending it when Bill Miller cleared his throat to get his attention. Carl looked up at the younger detective. "What?"

"Jesus, you look like shit," Miller opened with.

Carl nodded, "Thanks asshole," he said. "Did you need something?"

"Captain wants to see you in the situation room."

"The what?" Carl frowned.

"Oh yeah, while you were out he turned the small conference room into a regular epicenter of all things related to your case."

Carl sighed and pulled himself up from his desk. He picked up his paperwork and made his way down the hall. The small conference room had formerly been a store room for recent case files. With the addition of computers to the police force, the files had been digitized and archived in the basement. It now held a small conference table with a phone and a TV-VCR unit on a cart. As he walked in the room he saw D'Agostino and Devry pinning things up on a cork bulletin board that had been dragged into the room. The state lab guys were back from the hospital and were filling out reports at the table. The room was too small for this many people and Carl felt like he could barely breathe.

"Detective," D'Agostino said without turning around. He must have eyes in the back of his head. "We'll be running things out of here for now. It will be easier to pool our resources and spread things out."

"Sounds good," Carl responded, trying to sound enthusiastic without overdoing it.

D'Agostino turned away from the board and looked at Rick Emory from the state lab and asked, "Rick, how long before we get a result on the samples you took?"

Emory started to answer but Carl found his attention drift towards the board. He stepped up and looked at photos of the house on Pinehurst, copies of the coroner's report and a Polaroid of the woman who had been removed from the house. In the picture she was looking at the camera with the same vacant expression he had seen in person. There was something about the eyes though, a sadness that she was trying to keep the world from knowing about. He looked at the picture and thought about something that Stan Lewendowski, the Kolb's neighbor, had mentioned.

"Carl," he was suddenly aware that D'Agostino was calling his name and everyone else in the room was looking at him.

He looked at D'Agostino. "Is there anything you'd like to throw in here?" the captain asked.

"Ahh, yeah..." he said slowly. "Can I get a copy on this picture?"

TWENTY
WINTER, 1978

Nick Arnetto hadn't waited long to exact his revenge on Wayne Porzio. A week after the incident at the party, Porzio had come out to the student lot at lunchtime to find all four tires of his Pontiac Lemans slashed. Nick was immediately suspected and a hunting knife was found in his locker. He was expelled, arrested and the case was referred to family court. The judge didn't care for Nick's attitude and the fact that Nick's father couldn't afford to make restitution to Porzio so he sent him to the Juvenile Detention Center on East Ferry Street for ninety days.

Mike was initially reluctant to keep selling weed for Eddie, but Eddie convinced him to keep at it, advising caution and telling him to recruit a trustworthy accomplice. Larry was too nervous. His street hockey friend, Tim Burns, was low key and quiet. Mike pitched the idea to him and told him about the cut he would get and Tim agreed.

One day they were cutting lunch and walking down the path behind the junior high school when they came across Fat Jack and Itch.

"What's up Schitz?' Jack sneered as he approached.

"Fuck off," Mike answered.

"What did you say?" Jack said, stepping in front of Mike.

"I said, fuck off."

"I heard your pal Nick is locked up."

"Yeah?" Mike looked right into Jack's eyes. Out of the corner of his eye he saw Tim squaring up with Itch.

Jack said nothing and tried to return Mike's stare. He could see the sudden doubt in Jack's eyes. He knew he'd already won. He punched Jack in the chin and the larger boy rocked back on his heels. Mike rushed in, throwing punches as Jack backpedaled until he tripped over a tree root in the path. Mike was on top of him, throwing punches as Jack tried to cover up. Mike eventually got tired and pushed himself up off of Jack who rolled over in the mud. He looked back at a stunned Itch and a smirking Tim. "C'mon, let's go." Mike said.

After the party and the beat down, Eddie Kolb had Mike and Nick working out in his basement.

There was a weight bench and a heavy bag and Eddie offered tips on fighting and self-defense.

Once when Eddie thought the two weren't taking it seriously enough, he got out two sets of boxing gloves and sparred with them. Nick and Mike both took a beating from Eddie, who said that it was just as important to be able to "take a punch" as it was to give one.

A week later Mike came home from school and found his mother sitting on the couch in the living room, crying. She was holding a tissue to her mouth and looking down at what was left of the coffee table, which was lying in pieces on the floor. Mike looked down at his mother.

After a moment she looked up at him with red-rimmed eyes. She straightened herself up and said, "Your dad got in trouble at work."

"What did he do?" Mike asked.

His mother looked back at the floor and clutched the tissue

tightly. "His supervisor said he smelled alcohol on his breath and they suspended him."

Mike shook his head. He looked at his mother and asked, "Did he hit you?"

She looked up. "What? No, no he's just in a bad mood."

MID-JANUARY, AND NICK was coming home. Mike had mixed feelings about it. He knew Nick had issues and couldn't help it, but was starting to wonder if a continued friendship with him would get him in trouble too. He didn't have many friends and Nick, despite his temper and his poor judgement was probably his best friend. It was a bitter cold afternoon and there was a foot of snow on the ground as Mike made his way to the house on Meadow Place. After the previous winter it didn't seem that bad. Mike went to the side door and rang the bell for the lower flat. Nick's father came down the steps and opened the door. He looked tired. Before he went away, Nick had explained that his dad had taken a second job to try to keep up with alimony and child support payments.

"Oh, hey Mike. C'mon in. Nick's in the basement."

Mike walked in past Nick's dad and went down the basement steps. He found Nick sitting in an old armchair by the foosball table smoking a cigarette and looking at a magazine. The landlady's dryer was running and the basement smelled of lint and dampness. Mike walked up to where Nick sat and Nick turned towards him suddenly as if he were startled. Then Nick sat back in the chair and a look of relief came over his face.

"Hey," Mike said.

"Hey," Nick responded and stood up. He looked different. He looked taller and thinner and there was a v-shaped scar over his left eye. "You miss me?" Nick asked.

"Like I'd miss a hemorrhoid," Mike answered

Nick smiled and they shook hands. "Smoke?" he asked, offering the pack to Mike.

"Sure." Mike took the cigarette and the light that Nick offered and sat down on a stool.

Nick sat down again and looked at Mike. There was something different about him on the inside too, a weariness or worldliness that hadn't been there before.

"So how was it?" Mike asked.

Nick shook his head. "Pretty bad," he said through a plume of smoke.

Mike waited for Nick to continue. Nick looked down at the ground and after a moment continued, "Lot of fights, that kind of shit. Kids getting their shit stolen and fucked with."

He looked back up at Mike. "I heard a kid get raped."

"What?"

Nick shook his head slowly again. "The most fucked up thing I've ever heard. "This skinny kid from Amherst or somewhere. He used to cry in his bed at night. One day there was a fight in the cafeteria and two guys dragged him into the boys' room where I was and…" his voice trailed off.

"Holy shit!" Mike said quietly.

"Yeah, I hid in the stall until they were done and they just left him there. I took off and didn't say anything to anybody because that would have been bad."

"Shit," Mike said. He pointed at Nick's scar and asked, "Where did that come from."

"Third day there I got into it with some Puerto Rican kid trying to act all bad. I did alright though. He's got a couple of marks on him too."

"Fuck Nick...I'm sorry."

Nick glared at Mike. "Sorry for what? You didn't do anything."

"I mean..."

Nick cut him off, "It is what it is. After the fight and the other thing I learned to keep my head down."

Mike was struck silent. He couldn't imagine what Nick had gone through.

"What about you?" Nick's voice brought him back to the present. "How are things with Eddie?"

"Alright," Mike answered. "I've had Tim Burns watching my back and we're doing okay. As a matter of fact, though, Eddie said he wanted to see us when you got home."

Twenty-One

June 21, 1988

Carl had taken a copy of the picture to the rectory at Our Lady help of Christians on Union Road after he left the station the previous afternoon. After ringing the bell three times the door was finally answered by a short, heavy set, balding priest in his forties. The priest had given Carl an odd look at first. Carl could only imagine how bad he looked, hung over, sweating and tired, as the priest explained that the church secretary had left for the day. Carl flashed his badge and said it was a police matter. He had shown the priest the photo of the woman only to have the priest explain that he had only recently been installed at the parish and didn't recognize the woman in the photograph. He suggested that Carl contact Monsignor Burke who had recently stepped down due to health reasons and moved to a home for retired clergy in Tonawanda. Carl got back in his car. It was after Five PM and he was tired. He fought off the urge to stop at Otto's and made his way home to his apartment on French Avenue.

The next morning he was up early. He showered, shaved, trimmed his mustache and put on his best suit, the one he wore to court, and headed out to O'Hara Avenue in Tonawanda. It was hot and humid as it had been for the past few weeks. Despite the humidity, the rain never seemed to come and offer the relief that a storm would bring.

The Catholic Retirement home was a one story brick building tucked behind Cardinal O'Hara High school. It looked like whoever was doing the grounds keeping was trying to compensate for the lack of rain, but they were fighting a losing battle. Carl was relieved when he walked into the lobby that the building was air conditioned. After identifying himself to the middle-aged receptionist at the desk in the lobby he was told that Father Burke was in the day room and escorted down the corridor to a large, bright room with couches and armchairs. There were four men in the room, none of them in clerical garb. One of them, the one seated in an armchair closest to the door, looked to be sound asleep, possibly even dead Carl thought. He hoped that it wasn't Burke. The receptionist pointed toward another man, seated by the windows reading a newspaper. Carl thanked her and went over to him. As he approached, he noticed that the man had an oxygen tank next to him with a tube running up to his nose. He had a few wisps of hair combed across a balding scalp. Despite it being warm in the room, the old priest was wearing a cardigan

Carl cleared his throat. "Father Burke?"

Burke looked up at Carl and smiled, "Yes?"

"I'm Detective Carl Wisniewski. I'm with the Cheektowaga Police."

Burke raised his eyebrows and said, "Finally. You caught me."

"What?" Carl asked.

"Just kidding. I apologize. The boredom here makes me say silly things. How can I help you, Detective?"

Carl pointed at a chair near Burke's and asked, "I was wondering if I could ask you about a person who may have been a parishioner of yours."

"Of course, please sit down."

Carl showed Burke the picture and Burke studied it closely for a few minutes.

"Keep in mind that the lady in the picture has been hospitalized and is currently not in the best frame of mind," Carl prompted. "She's been living like a hermit for a while and her appearance might have changed since you last saw her."

Burke looked up at Carl. "I see," he said. "I was at Our Lady Help of Christians for eighteen years and the parish changed quite a bit in that time. I did try to get to know my parishioners as well as I could. People came and went, and then you had the twice a year crowd."

"The twice a year crowd?"

"Christmas and Easter," Burke answered. "Part-time Catholics we called them," he added with a smirk. He looked back down at the picture. "But the regulars..." he trailed off.

Carl waited patiently. Burke stared at the picture intently for another moment and then said, "I have to say she looks familiar. If it's who I think it may be, you were right about her living rough. The poor thing looks like she's been put through the ringer."

Carl explained the situation that the woman had been found in and that she may have been part of his congregation. "Any idea on a name Father?" he added.

Burke let his hand with the photo fall into his lap and looked up at nothing in particular. "If it's who I think it is she was a regular at the eight o'clock mass every Sunday. She had a husband and a son who attended our school." He looked back at Carl. "As I remember it she usually came to church alone. I met the husband once or twice and forgive me, but he was an unpleasant man."

"And the son?"

"I don't remember but I think he transferred to Maryvale before

eighth grade for some reason. I think he made his First Commu-
nion but I don't remember him being confirmed."

Carl was starting to wonder if this trip had been for nothing.
How accurate was the old priest's memory? What if he was thinking about someone other than the lady in the picture? And he still
didn't have what he came for.

"Any thought on a name?" Carl asked.

Burke closed his eyes. "Mary," he said after a moment.

Carl had his notebook out and hoped that Burke wasn't finished.

"Something German," Burke continued, opening his eyes.
Schmitt, Schuler, Schneider." He shook his head. "I'm sorry Detective. It's not coming back to me."

"No Father," Carl said rising. "This gives me something to go on.
I can't thank you enough."

He offered his hand to Burke who took it in his hand and shook
it. Carl turned to leave and Burke called out to him, "Detective
Wisniewski?"

Carl turned around. "Yes."

"I hope you find out who she is. More importantly I hope that
you find someone to take care of her."

Carl had to admit to himself that he hadn't thought about the
woman like that to this point. She was alone, confused and scared
and a ward of the state. "I'll do my best, Father."

TWENTY-TWO
APRIL 1978

MIKE COULD TELL Nick was angrier than ever. Not on the surface. He hid it well. But he smiled infrequently and Mike knew that under the surface Nick was mad at the world. Nick had been sent to an "Alternative" high school that the county ran in Amherst. It was a no-nonsense, no freedom situation for "at risk" students who had been deemed too unruly for their original schools. Expectations were low and the workload was easy, but that didn't mean that most of the kids there would finish the program. For his part, Mike had been pulling passing grades and keeping a low profile at school. He had to admit that it was easier without Nick around during the school day. He was still selling weed for Eddie Kolb. Tim Burns had proven to be a capable accomplice. He was quiet and discreet. He made a good lookout and knew his place.

Things at home hadn't gotten much better. As soon as Mike's father got off his suspension he mysteriously hurt his back and was out on disability. He was home all the time. Mike could see his mother walking on eggshells and spent as much time away from home as possible.

Mike and Nick still hung out after school and on weekends. One weekend in April Nick announced that his father was going on a fishing trip and he was going to have a party. That Friday Mike made his way to Nick's house at 7:30. Nick had already started drinking, something he had been doing more of since he got home. He had procured a case of beer from somewhere and he had liberated a bottle of Black Velvet whiskey from his father's liquor cabinet. At least Nick seemed happy for the time being. He offered Mike a hit off of a joint he had lit and put an AC/DC cassette in his father's tape deck. Larry, Tim and a few other guys from the neighborhood arrived shortly after. At about 8:30 the doorbell rang and a few girls from school walked in. They all sat in the living room, smoking and drinking.

Mike lost track of time, his head was buzzing. He found himself sitting on the couch next to a girl named Debbie that he vaguely knew from school. He had never spoken to her before but she sat there talking to him like they were old friends. He was half listening to what she said. He was watching Nick and Debbie's friend, Kathy Sharp, making out on the recliner. The music was loud and the room was stuffy. After a while, Nick and Kathy stood up and headed off into Nick's room. No one else seemed to notice, or at least acknowledge Nick's departure. There was a quarters game going on in the kitchen and the others were caught up in watching the game, with the exception of Larry, who had passed out in an armchair in the corner.

Mike looked at Debbie who was looking directly into his eyes. "What?" he said.

She laughed. "I didn't say anything," she replied. She was still staring into his eyes. She was tall and thin with large brown eyes and was wearing blue eyeshadow. Up close Mike could make out the acne scars that she had tried to cover up with makeup. She leaned in and kissed him on the mouth. A second later he could feel her tongue in his mouth and he reciprocated. He was aware that he had become aroused, and shifted his weight to ease the strain. It didn't help matters when he felt her hand on his thigh.

She broke off the kiss and stood up. Mike's head was spinning. He looked up at her, standing over him and she extended her hand, "C'mon," she said.

Mike awkwardly stood up and took her hand. She led him through the kitchen. Tim Burns looked up from the quarters game and raised his eyebrows. No one else seemed to react or said anything as they went out the door and down the steps to the basement. There was an old couch near the foosball table. Debbie led Mike to it and pushed him down. She went back over to the steps and turned the lights off. The only light in the basement was coming through the windows from outside. He could barely make out her shadow moving back towards him. Then she was back on the couch and they were kissing again. He could feel her bra through the sweater she was wearing as she pulled herself closer. He felt lightheaded, like he had the flu but he kissed her back and moved his hand to the front of her sweater. He felt her pulling at his belt and then the buckle gave way. Something was wrong, he felt like he wasn't in control of his body anymore. He'd kissed a few girls before but this was the real deal. She roughly unbuttoned his jeans and pulled the zipper down and it happened.

"Jesus Christ," he heard her say.

His body had just finished shuddering when the lights snapped on. At the foot of the stairs was the landlady with a laundry basket on her hip and a shocked expression on her face.

That effectively ended the party. The landlady pounded on the door to the flat until someone had the sense to turn the music down and get Nick out of his room. She was livid, telling Nick that he was lucky she didn't call the police, let alone tell his dad. To his credit, Nick remained polite and contrite with the old woman. He apologized and told her the party was over. Mike remained in the basement until the landlady had gone back upstairs and discreetly went into the bathroom to clean himself up. When he came out of the bathroom. Everyone was gone except for Nick. He was smirking and as soon as he saw Mike, he burst out laughing.

MIKE DIDN'T SPEAK to Nick until the following weekend. On Friday Nick called him and told him he needed to stock up for the following week. Mike curtly agreed and they agreed to meet at Mike's house at seven O'clock.

Mike's father was in a foul mood. He'd spent the afternoon in his "workshop" in the basement and had taken his dinner downstairs instead of eating with Mike and his mother. Mike couldn't wait to get out of the house. When Mike was putting on his jacket, his father came up from the basement. "Where you goin'?' he asked suspiciously. "Over to Larry's," Mike responded.

His father looked at him. "You need a goddamned haircut." he said. He went to the refrigerator and got another Genny. Mike didn't wait for any further conversation. He was out the back door and briskly walking down the driveway. It was already past seven and no sign of Nick. He decided to walk down Clover Place towards Meadow and hopefully meet Nick on the way. He got all the way to the corner and turned right onto Meadow. Still no Nick. He walked up to Nick's house and stood at the end of the driveway. Nick's father's car was parked out front and he could see a light on in the lower flat, but he hesitated. Something told him not to go to the door. He wasn't sure what he was afraid of, except for possibly reliving last weekend's disaster. He passed the house and turned right onto Genesee Street instead. He walked up the I-90 overpass and found Nick, sitting on the metal stairs that led from the bus stop on the overpass down to Pinehurst. Nick was drinking out of a bottle in a paper bag.

"Hey," Mike announced himself as he ascended the stairs. No response from Nick. He got closer to Nick and tapped him on the shoulder. Nick flinched a bit and turned his head up towards Mike. His hair was a mess and he had the beginnings of a bruise on his left cheek.

"Shit, what happened to you?" Mike asked.

Nick looked down and said, "Got into it with the old man today. The old bag told him about the party and he lost his mind."

Mike walked down a few more steps and turned to face Nick. Nick's eyes were red, either from drinking or crying. Mike had never seen Nick cry. He didn't think he was capable. "I'm sorry man," Mike said. "It's my fault."

Nick laughed and teetered to his left. "Nah, she was going to complain anyway. Even before she saw your dick explode."

Mike grimaced. He had hoped Nick would have let the incident go, but at the same time he felt bad for his friend. "C'mon," Mike said. "You can't stay here."

Nick stood up and almost fell down on top of Mike. He righted himself and they walked on to the Kolb's.

Glenda answered the back door wearing a flannel shirt and jeans. Her hair was pulled back and her eyes were clear. She explained that Eddie had gone to Canada "on business" but he had left a few bags of weed to resupply them. She told them to wait at the door.

"Um…" Mike cleared his throat.

"What?" Glenda responded, turning back towards him.

"Um, I was wondering if we could come in for a while."

She frowned but smiled at the same time. "What for?" she asked.

Mike glanced back at Nick. "Um, Nick's not feeling so good right now…"

Glenda looked at Nick who was swaying slightly and looking at nothing in particular. "So he's fucked up." She frowned again.

"I'm fine," Nick murmured.

"And he can't go home like this," Mike added more assertively. "His father's already pissed at him."

Glenda thought for a moment and then said, "Alright, but just for an hour or so. I'm not running a rehab center."

They went into the living room and sat down. As usual it smelled of cigarettes and the radio was tuned to one of the local rock stations. Nick flopped down in the recliner and fished out a pack of mostly crushed cigarettes from his jacket pocket. He pulled a clearly broken cigarette and fumbled for his lighter.

"Well, while you're here, I guess I should offer refreshments," she said with a bit of sarcasm. She left the room and a moment later came back with a glass of vodka for herself and two cans of Coke.

"Beer?" Nick slurred.

She laughed, her eyes lighting up. "I don't think so."

Nick mumbled something inaudible.

"So why is your old man mad at you?" she asked.

Nick stopped fumbling with his lighter and looked at her. "Had a party last weekend," he said. "Everything was fine until the landlady walked in on Romeo over there premature ejarcul...ejac..." he burst out laughing. "He jizzed in his pants," he managed to get out and started laughing again.

Mike could feel his face flush. He wanted to cross the room and punch Nick right in his face but he was too embarrassed to move. Nick sat back in the recliner and closed his eyes. Mike glanced at Glenda, who was thankfully glaring at Nick. After a moment she turned to him.

"Why do you hang out with this asshole?" she asked.

Mike shrugged. He didn't know how to put it into words. The beginning strains of "Layla" by Derrick and the Dominos came on the radio. Glenda shook her head and said, "I love this song." She stood up and went over to the stereo to turn the volume up. Mike looked at Nick, who had clearly passed out. The broken cigarette had fallen to the floor.

Glenda came back to the couch and sat down next to Mike. Mike felt warm all over again and looked at her sideways.

"It happens," she said. "You're not the first one."

This was not a conversation Mike wanted to have with anyone. He took a sip of his Coke and looked at his feet. He could smell her, a combination of cigarettes, vodka and some kind of perfumed soap.

"As a matter of fact, it's a good thing," she added.

He looked at her quizzically. She was just a few feet away from him and her blue eyes were shining. "It just means you're a healthy young man. How old are you?"

"Sixteen," he answered. He didn't know if he had said it audibly but she must have understood because she nodded.

"You just need to relax." With that, she took a joint out of the pocket of her shirt and lit it. It only took a moment to feel the effect. The instrumental part of the song had started and he could feel some of the tension leave his body.

"You're a good guy," she said. "Don't let that asshole bring you down." She leaned over and kissed him on the cheek. His head was swimming and he was nervous. But part of him wanted to stay on that couch forever.

Twenty-Three

CARL WAS RACING down I-290 back towards Cheektowaga. He'd borrowed the phone at the reception desk at the retired priest's residence and placed a call to Captain D'Agostino and told him about his interview with Father Burke. It wasn't much, but it was something. D'Agostino agreed to have Bill Miller take a break from his shoplifting case and get a map of the parish and then head to the town assessor's office and start cross-referencing it with tax records with German sounding names in the area. He could picture Miller puffing out his cheeks at the task he'd been given. Who knew how many families had those names in an area populated by the descendants of German and Eastern European immigrants. Carl told D'Agostino he would be back to help Miller as soon as possible but there was one more stop he had to make. The Captain had hesitated at first. Carl sensed that D'Agostino wanted to ask more questions but at the end, let him off the hook to do his own thing. At least he trusted Carl enough now not to micromanage all his movements.

Twenty minutes later he pulled up in front of Bob Czerczak's house on Woodbine. Carl had to find out what Bob hadn't told him about his comings and goings at the Kolb house and wasn't going to leave until the old cop told him the truth. This might be his last chance to talk to Bob without involving Devry or anyone else on the case. The sun was beating down now and Carl stripped off his jacket and tossed it in the back seat. Czerczak's house was dark and the shades were down. He walked briskly up the driveway, climbed the single step to the front door and leaned into the doorbell. No answer. He knocked loudly on the storm door. There was no way Czerczak could have not heard him. Was the old man playing possum again? He knocked again and got frustrated, beads of sweat had formed on his forehead. He stepped off the stoop and walked over to the attached garage. He was peering in and saw the top of the car in the gloom of the garage. "God dammit!" he said.

"Can I help you?" came a voice from behind him.

Carl turned around and saw a thin, elderly man at the foot of the driveway. The man looked at the gun and badge on Carl's hip and a concerned look crossed his face.

"I'm looking for Mr. Czerczak," Carl said. "I'm a former coworker of his and I was just checking in."

The old man looked at Carl with some skepticism. Carl knew that his demeanor must not have suggested that this was a social visit.

"Bob's not here," the old man said.

Carl tried to soften his demeanor. "Oh, do you know where he went?"

The man seemed to consider whether he should tell Carl anything at all but finally said, "He left yesterday. Said he was going to visit his boy in California. He asked me if I could pick up his mail."

Carl nodded and tried to smile but realized it was probably closer to a grimace. He thought about giving the man a business card but then thought that it might do more harm than good. He had no idea what was going through Czerczak's mind right now so maybe the less said the better. "Okay," he said. "Did he say how long he'd be gone for?"

"Nope," the old man replied.

Carl thanked him and went back to the car. In the rearview mirror he saw the old man watching him as he pulled away down the street.

Could it be a coincidence that Czerczak decided to fly across the country right now? In his gut Carl thought otherwise. Now, not only did he have to find out who the lady in the County Home was, he also had to find Bob Czerczak.

Twenty-Four
Spring 1978

Mike and Glenda sat on the couch talking for another hour until Nick stirred and Mike thought it was safe to take him home. Nick surprised Mike the next day when he called and apologized. He said he had patched things up with his dad and he thanked Mike for looking out for him. The incident at the party was never mentioned again. Just before school let out for the summer Mike got another surprise. Debbie, the girl from the party, came up to Mike in the hallway and gave him a slip of paper with her phone number. He had braced himself when she approached him, ready to be further humiliated, but she acted like nothing had happened and told him to call her and hang out on summer vacation.

Eddie came back from Canada and was spending a lot of time with Spider and Tony. Mike knew something was up but he and Nick weren't included in whatever was going on. That was fine with him. He was sixteen and had signed up for Driver's Ed, and the money he made slinging weed for Eddie Kolb didn't go very far. He had applied for a few jobs and was called for an interview at Top's Market on Genesee Street. He reluctantly went, hoping the manager didn't recognize him from the cigarette buying incident from the previous year. His mother had fussed over him before the interview, picking out a clean shirt and smoothing down his hair. Fortunately he was interviewed by a young assistant manager and was hired to push carts and sort deposit bottles three nights a week. Nick's father got Nick a job at the warehouse where he worked in Depew.

Mike's father was still on disability but things had taken a turn for the worse. The railroad was acquired by another company and they were closing down operations at the Central Terminal.

Technically he had no job to go back to when his disability ran out. The union was treading water. There were only so many jobs to go around and it was looking grim. Mike saw his mother trying hard to put on a brave face. She was acting like nothing was wrong but underneath Mike could sense the strain. One night that summer Mike got home from work and found his mother crying over a cup of tea in the kitchen. When he asked her what was wrong, she said nothing, changed the subject and then went off to bed. The next morning, his father emerged from the basement with a swollen lip and a surly attitude. For once he didn't lay into Mike. He got a cup of coffee and quietly retreated back downstairs.

The summer flew by. Mike picked up as many shifts as possible at the store and was putting money away every week. He and Nick were still selling the occasional bag of weed but Eddie's interest in the enterprise seemed to be flagging. The few times they went to the Kolb's house, things seemed tense. Glenda never seemed to be around and they were usually resupplied and then shown the door.

He called Debbie and they went out a few times. There were some make out sessions and some petting but Mike was still extremely nervous when things got heated. Debbie never pushed him though and in the end she seemed to lose interest.

FALL 1978

THE SCHOOL YEAR had begun. Mike was taking auto repair at the vocational center as well as his core classes. He still enjoyed working with his hands over sitting in a classroom and was excelling at it. Nick, on the other hand, was causing problems at his alternative school. He was on the verge of being expelled when his father relented and let him drop out. He went to work full time at the warehouse.

By October Mike had saved over five hundred dollars and with his mother's help, bought a 1970 Chevy Caprice. It had some rust on it and it ran rough when he turned the motor. He knew that he would be able to work on it at the vocational center though and bought it. He went to the cut-rate insurance place on Bailey Avenue and after a two hour ordeal at the DMV he was on the road. His father was not pleased. He complained that Mike's car would be in the way and it had a small oil leak, so Mike would have to leave it in the street.

With Mike and Nick being less than welcome at the Kolb's they decided to pool their resources and get a set of weights for themselves. They bought a bench a few bars and weights, pushed the foosball table out of the way and had a workout space in Nick's basement. Mike soon realized he had to get to Nick early, before he started imbibing if he wanted to get a decent workout in. Nick was trying hard to act like a grown up now that he had left school behind. He was just confused about what that meant and didn't seem to have any boundaries. Mike could sense that underneath the bravado, Nick was hurting. He just didn't know how to help him except to be there for him and try to rein in his more harmful behaviors.

SPRING 1980

TWO SCHOOL YEARS had come and gone and Mike was graduating from high school. His father's workman's comp claim had dragged on for almost the whole time with a settlement finally being reached. A check was cut, lawyer's fees were deducted and his father at age fifty-one, was out of work. He took a job as a cashier at the gas station at the corner of Union Road and Genesee Street. Even though he won his settlement he was bitter. Mike wondered how his father thought it would all play out and why his father couldn't seem to move on.

Graduation was a low key affair. Mike's mother wanted to have a party, but his father's mood and attitude made it out of the question. Mike made the rounds of other people's parties after commencement with some of his friends. Some were off to college. Tim Burns had joined the army and was headed to boot camp in a few weeks. Mike wanted nothing to do with any kind of continuing education. He had learned all he was going to at school. He had already started applying to every auto repair shop and dealership in the area.

He was also ready to leave Eddie Kolb and his business behind. Two things held him back from making a clean break; Nick was still into it and Mike didn't want to desert him, and he was worried about Glenda. In fact, he thought about her all the time.

Twenty-Five
June 21, 1988

Carl arrived at the station just before noon. Captain D'Agostino informed him that he had already responded to his request and sent Miller, Devry and a patrolman to the Assessor's office at the old Town Hall next door to start searching for "German sounding" names located within the Our Lady Help of Christian's parish. Carl went to join them and as he walked across the hot blacktop couldn't stop thinking about Bob Czerczak and his disappearing act.

They were set up in a room in the stuffy basement of Town Hall. The patrolman, a young guy Carl barely recognized, was bringing boxes into the room. Miller had put a map of the town on a bulletin board and demarcating the borders of the parish on it with a thick black marker. Devry had already dove into the first box of records and had a binder open in front of him at a folding table in the center of the room.

"Okay," Carl said rolling up his sleeves. "We're looking for tax records and real estate transactions for a likely name within the parish. Will start with '86 and go back five years, then go back farther if we have to. Our best guess is that our Jane Doe, or Mary, is between fifty and sixty years of age." He walked over to the open box on the table and took a binder out. He pulled his notebook out of his back pocket and opened it to a clean page

Miller had finished with the map. He walked to the table and said, "Not to be negative or anything like that, but what if the priest was wrong about the name?"

Without looking up from the binder in front of him Carl said, "Then we're fucked and this was a giant waste of time."

Miller picked a binder out of the box and pulled his notebook out of his coat pocket.

Two hours later they had a list of over thirty possible names. They ruled out, at least for the time being, any one that was either too young or too old to be their Jane Doe. Carl went to the map and started marking addresses that the other three called out. They were going to have to do a lot of follow up to eliminate the possibilities. Carl was standing back looking at the map when the young patrolman cleared his throat. "Almost missed this one sir." he said.

"Go ahead," Carl said, stepping back up to the map.

"A house sold by Arthur and Mary Schultz in '86, 11 Clover Place."

Carl looked at the map and zeroed in on the address. "Mother fucker," He said.

"What is it? Devry asked.

"That's right around the corner from the Kolb's."

What he didn't say out loud was that the house was also right across the street from Bob Czerczak.

TWENTY-SIX
SEPTEMBER 8, 1980

"So WHAT HAPPENED?" Mike asked.

Nick was sitting in the passenger seat looking straight ahead. Mike had picked him up from the warehouse on George Urban Boulevard where Nick had worked, until that day. Nick lit a cigarette and rolled down his window. "The foreman had it out for me," he said.

"What do you mean?"

Nick spat out the window and said, "The fucking forklift driver spilled a pallet and said that I didn't wrap it right, so of course the prick foreman gets in my face and says I'm not worth the trouble. He starts going on about all the times I came in late or took too long on my breaks. So I told him to shove the job up his ass."

"Shit Nick, what did your dad say?"

Nick looked out the window and in a quieter voice said, "I don't know. He wasn't on the dock when it happened."

That can't be good, Mike thought. Nick had said that his dad was always telling him not to embarrass him at work and their relationship had been strained by Nick's behavior in general since he had dropped out of school. They rode in silence for a while. Nick had called Mike at his job at the dealership where Mike was actually doing well. He'd worked hard and ingratiated himself with the service manager. He went from lot boy to tire changer and was now also doing inspections and minor repairs. Nick's call came at a slow time. It was a Friday, the bays were empty and the manger let him leave an hour early to collect his friend.

"We need to go see Eddie," Nick said suddenly.

"What? Why?"

Nick looked over at Mike and said, "You know why. We need to move up from selling nickel and dime bags and start making money."

Mike knew he was referring to Eddie's cocaine business, which Eddie had yet to even discuss with them. "I don't know..."

"You don't know?" Nick cut him off. "He's making money off that shit. We're not kids anymore, Schultz. We need to move up too."

Mike shook his head. "Look, I'm sorry you lost your job. . ."

"Fuck that place," Nick cut him off again. "I'm talking about making real money, not working at a shit job or being a grease monkey like you the rest of my life."

They had just passed the Union Road intersection and Mike had heard enough. He pulled into the backlot of the Airport Plaza and slammed on the brakes. Nick was glaring at him and he glared right back. "You say we're not kids anymore, so when the fuck are you going to grow up?"

"What the fuck does that mean?" Nick replied.

"You lost your job, got kicked out of two schools. All because you act like a fucking child!"

"Fuck you!" Nick said, shaking his head.

Mike wasn't finished, "Now you want to go over to Eddie's house and tell him you want in on his coke business? How do you think that's gonna go?"

Nick had his hand on the door handle and looked like he was about to bolt from the car. Mike was seething and more than ready to let him do so. After a moment Nick's hand fell from the handle and he looked straight ahead. Another moment passed and he said, "You're right." His face was scrunched up and he looked like he was in pain. Mike's own rage was starting to ebb.

Nick rubbed his temples with his fingers and tried to surreptitiously wipe his eyes. "Look," he said. "I know you've got your own thing going on. I'm not asking you to get involved. It's, just, it's just that I feel like I don't have a lot of options, you know?"

"Fuck," Mike muttered. He put the car in gear and pulled back onto Genesee Street.

Nick didn't want to go home in case his father was looking for him. Mike avoided family dinners at his house due to his father's ill temper. He felt like he was deserting his mother at times, but the prospect of listening to the old man bitch about anything and everything was daunting. They decided to go to La Bella Sicilia on the other side of the Thruway for pizza and to form a plan on how to approach Eddie.

It was almost seven o'clock when Mike drove past his house on the way to the Kolb's. His Father's car was in the driveway and the lights were out with the exception of the bluish glow from the television in the living room. It all looked depressingly normal. They rounded the corner and pulled up in front of the Kolb's. Eddie's Dodge was in the driveway as well as a small pickup truck that belonged to Eddie's friend Tony. They got out and walked up the drive to the back door. Eddie answered after they knocked, dressed in a flannel shirt and jeans.

"There they are!" he said cheerfully. "Get in here you rascals."

The music was loud as usual. "Go on in and I'll get you guys a beer," he said gesturing towards the living room. Tony was seated on a chair in his usual spot in the living room. He nodded at them when they walked in. Mike couldn't remember hearing Tony say more than a few words at a time since he'd met him. Eddie came in and handed out the beer. "Have a seat," he said.

Glenda came part way down the stairs. She looked ashen and her hair was a mess. "Eddie," she said, her voice barely audible over the music.

Eddie looked at her and said, "What's up babe?"

"I have such a fucking headache."

Eddie walked over to the stereo and turned the volume down. He looked back at her and took a pull on his beer. Without a word she turned and went back up the stairs. He sat in the recliner and looked over at Mike and Nick on the couch. "What's up lads? Do you need to resupply?"

Mike looked at Nick who looked uncharacteristically unsure of himself. Nick was obviously not going to initiate the conversation so he spoke up, "We appreciate the stuff you've done for us..." Mike started, his voice faltering. He wasn't ready to have this conversation with Eddie either.

Eddie smirked. "But?" he asked.

"We wanted to help you with the other thing."

Eddie laughed out loud and looked at Tony who just sat there stoically as usual.

"The other thing?" Eddie asked, faking confusion.

"The coke," Nick said flatly.

"Boys, boys, boys." Eddie said. "I don't know what you're talking about."

"Cut the shit," Nick said. "We're offering to help you. You know you can trust us."

Eddie's face darkened. "Listen, you little shit. This isn't for a couple of kids. We're not talking about some bullshit possession charge for holding a nickel bag of weed, alright." He shook his head. He glared at them and Mike felt like crawling under the couch.

They heard the back door open and footsteps across the kitchen. Eddie's friend, Spider, entered the room. His lank hair was greasy and it looked like he hadn't slept in several days.Eddie looked at Spider and said, "And where the fuck have you been?"

"Busy," Spider said.

Eddie stood up. "Busy? Too busy to answer your phone?"

Spider shifted from foot to foot. Even though it looked like he hadn't slept in days, he had a nervous energy. "What the fuck you want me to say man?"

"And the five hundred you were short?"

"I told you I'd get it," Spider whined.

Eddie walked over to Spider who was trying to look brave and sure of himself. Eddie had at least six inches and fifty pounds on him so he was mostly failing.

"That was last week," Eddie said. "What's your excuse this week?"

"C'mon man," Spider said, breaking eye contact and looking down at the floor.

Eddie lowered his voice. "I told you this wasn't going to work if you started sampling the product."

"I'm not..." Spider stammered.

"The fuck you aren't," Eddie said, jabbing his finger into Spider's chest.

"What about your old lady?" Spider protested. "How much shit has..."

In a flash Eddie brought his other hand up and broke his beer bottle across the side of Spider's head. Spider fell in a heap and after a moment started making sounds like a wounded animal. Eddie's hand was bleeding from the broken bottle. He bent over and wiped it on Spider's leather jacket. He grabbed Spider by the hair with his undamaged hand and dragged him out of the room into the kitchen. Tony stood up and gestured for Mike and Nick to follow.

Spider was howling now. He was swearing and alternately saying he was sorry and then in the next breath saying he was going to kill Eddie. Out of the corner of his eye Mike saw Glenda enter the kitchen doorway and take in the scene, impassively at first and then she seemed to process what was happening and she looked upset. He wanted to escort her out of the room and tell her it was all going to be over soon but he couldn't move.

"Mike! Nick" Eddie yelled over his shoulder. He had Spider on his feet with a hand over his mouth. Spider looked like he was on the verge of passing out. "You want to help me?" Eddie said. "Get this piece of shit out of here. I don't care where, just someplace far away. I don't need my asshole neighbor calling the cops again."

They looked at each other. Mike wanted to be anywhere else right now and he sensed that Nick felt the same. They grabbed Spider under his arms and walked him out to Mike's car. Spider was semi-conscious, probably from a combination of the drugs and the blow to the head and offered little resistance. They loaded him into the back of the car and sped off into the night.

"What the fuck are we supposed to do with him?" Mike asked.

"How the fuck should I know," Nick shot back. He reached into the back seat and slapped Spider across the face. "Hey asshole!"

Spider just mumbled and his head lolled back and then fell forward. Nick looked at his hand which now had Spider's blood on it. "Goddamn it," he said. He reached back and grabbed a handful of Spider's hair. "Wake up asshole!" he screamed. "Where do you live?"

"Ti...Tiorunda," Spider managed. Tiorunda was a neighborhood in Cheektowaga that was mostly comprised of apartments that had been built as temporary housing for factory workers during World

War II. After the war, with the area's increase in population as the city and surrounding suburbs expanded in the industrial boom, the buildings were always occupied and had never been replaced. The buildings, which were sparse and cheaply constructed, resembled military barracks more than apartments. Still they stood, poorly maintained but inexpensive to rent. They had also turned into one of the poorest neighborhoods in the county, and with the poverty came drugs and crime. The town had changed the name of the area to Cedar Grove Heights in the hope that it would lose some of the negativity associated with the name, but at its heart it would always be Tiorunda.

"Where in Tiorunda?" Mike yelled over his shoulder as he sped over the I-90 overpass.

"Who fucking cares." Nick said, facing forward in his seat again. "We'll drop him off at the drive in."

Then they heard the unmistakable sound of Spider vomiting in the back of Mike's car.

A few minutes later they were at the gate of the Buffalo Drive-In on Harlem Road. The drive-in sat on the edge of Tiorunda and was closed for the season. Mike turned off the headlights and took a second to look around to make sure no one else was around. The smell from whatever Spider had thrown up was overpowering. Mike felt himself gag as he climbed out of the car. It was one of those early autumn nights where you could smell fall coming but the humidity of summer was lingering. Mike looked over the roof of the car. Nick had already pushed his seat up and was pulling Spider out of the car by the lapels of his jacket.

"Fuck," Nick said. "I've got puke on me."

Mike walked around the car. Nick had pushed Spider back into the side of the car and Spider had somehow managed to stay upright. "You're home asshole," Nick hissed.

"Fuckin' Eddie," Spider hissed.

"Get the fuck off my car!" Mike growled, trying not to raise his voice.

Spider stood up unsteadily. "He's going to fuck you too," he said pointing at Nick.

"Do you remember the first time we met?" Nick asked him.

Spider frowned and looked confused. "Huh?"

Nick swung his fist and it connected with Spider's jaw. He went down in a heap. Just as Mike thought Nick was going to break off and get back in the car he kicked Spider in the face, with the sickening crunch of cartilage as his boot connected with Spider's nose.

"Fuck Nick! That's enough."

Blood was pouring out of Spiders nose and he lay groaning on the asphalt. Mike saw Nick's expression in the dim light. It was an odd combination of satisfaction and fear, relief and guilt. Nick smiled suddenly and said, "Yeah, let's go."

They rode in silence back to Meadow Place. Mike stopped in front of Nick's house and Nick wordlessly got out of the car and slowly walked up the driveway. Mike pulled away, wondering if Nick's father was up waiting for him.

It was just before midnight when Mike pulled into his own driveway. He inched the car up behind his father's and turned the engine off. Even though he had rolled all the windows down he could still smell Spider's sick. The house was dark except for a dim light coming from one of the basement windows. The driveway was illuminated by a floodlight that Mike's father had installed over the garage door. Mike went to the garage, retrieved a bucket and some rags and took it to the spigot on the back of the house.

He leaned into the passenger side door and was mopping up the vomit in the back seat. He had to fight the urge to throw up himself but after a while he was making headway on the mess.

As he was just about finished he felt a sharp blow to his backside. He quickly stood up and saw his father, standing unsteadily looking at him. He realized his father had just kicked him.

"What'd I tell you about parking this piece of shit in my driveway?" The irony of this was that Mike's car was only two years older than his dad's and he kept it in better shape.

"I was just about to move it."

His father stepped closer to look into the car. He reeked of alcohol and cigarettes. He looked back up at Mike and asked, "What the hell are you doin' anyway?"

"Somebody got sick in the back seat."

His father snorted. "Was it that punk Nick you run around with?"

"No."

His father looked at him. "I know what you're doing," he said. "I know about the drugs and the booze, you little shit. You're not fooling anyone."

Mike was tired and his head was starting to throb. He walked around to the driver's side of the car. His father was right on his heels. "Don't you walk away when I'm talking to you." his father grabbed Mike by the shoulder and turned him around.

"What?" Mike growled, "Are you going to give me some fatherly advice now?"

His father went to slap him but Mike caught him by the wrist with his left and then he brought his right up and grabbed his father by the throat. He pushed him up against the side of the house. His father struggled for a moment. Between the weight lifting and working with his hands and arms Mike had grown stronger than he realized. His father hit Mike in the side of the head with his free left hand. Mike saw red for a second and then pulled his father away from the house only to slam him back up against it again.

His father tried to pull Mike's hand off his throat in vain. Their faces were inches apart.

"That's the last time you lay a hand on me, you piece of shit."

His father was gasping for air and Mike realized he was squeezing his windpipe. He eased up his grip and pushed himself off. His father leaned over, coughing and gagging for a few minutes. He finally straightened up and took a step back. He pointed at Mike.

"Get out!" he screamed hoarsely. "You're out! Get your ass out of here and don't come back or I'll call the cops!"

Mike took a step towards his father who almost fell over backwards retreating. "Fine, but if I find out you lay a hand on mom again I'll fucking kill you!"

His father, red-faced, turned and went to the back door of the house. Mike steadied his breath and got into his car. He didn't know where he was going to go but he knew it was time to leave. He pulled back out of the driveway and put the car in drive. As he stepped on the accelerator he thought he saw the ex-cop, looking at him from his yard across the street.

TWENTY-SEVEN

JUNE 21, 1988

It was just after 4:00pm and they had all gathered back in the makeshift situation room. Carl was somewhat surprised to see that they had been joined by Chief Kopasz, who was standing behind Captain D'Agostino. Carl himself was standing, he finally felt like the investigation was gaining some traction and was too amped to sit.

"How many women fit the profile?" D'Agostino asked.

Devry spoke up, "After we eliminated the ones who didn't fit the profile, we can currently account for only four."

"And Carl, you have a favorite?" D'Agostino added.

"Yes sir, Mary Schultz, formerly of 11 Clover Place. She and her husband sold the house two years ago and so far we haven't found a forwarding address."

D'Agostino sat back in his chair and exhaled. "What do we know about the Shultz's?"

"I had Miller pull up the last census data from '80. It was a couple. Mary born in '33, Arthur born in '34 and one son," Carl checked his notebook, "Michael, born in '62."

"Alright," D'Agostino said. "What do you want to do next?"

"We need to confirm that our Jane Doe is in fact Mary Shultz." Carl said. "I'd like to have Miller and maybe someone else find any medical or dental records they can dig up on her and share it with the staff at the County Home. I don't know if it would be worth interviewing her again. Maybe see if she responds to the name."

"Could be worth a shot," Chief Kopasz said.

Carl looked at Devry. "Jeff, I know it's a long ride to Alden..."

Devry nodded. "No problem." He checked his watch. "If I leave now I can get there by five."

"Thanks," Carl went on. "I also want to track down the bank and the attorneys who handled the sale of the house. See if they have anything useful."

"You might not have much luck with that until business hours tomorrow," D'Agostino said.

"True," Carl replied. "In the meantime I want to go back and see if the Schultz's former neighbors have anything to offer."

"Sounds good," D'Agostino said. "Take Miller with you."

Miller raised his head at the mention of his name. D'Agostino looked at him. "Is that a problem, Detective?"

"No Sir," Miller answered.

D'Agostino stood up.

"Okay gentlemen. Let's get to it. Carl, if anything comes up, call dispatch and have them get a hold of me, any time. I don't care how late it is."

Carl nodded. "Yes sir," he said.

D'Agostino left the room, followed by the chief and Devry. Carl was pulling on his jacket when Miller caught his eye.

"What?" Carl said.

Miller looked at his watch. "I don't mean to complain Wiz..."

"But?"

"I have a softball game at 6:30 and..."

"You want to ditch a murder investigation for a softball game."

"It's not like that," Miller sputtered.

"Don't worry about it," Carl said. "I'm just busting balls. I'm just looking for a little background. I think I can handle it."

Miller looked relieved and a little embarrassed. "Thanks Carl."

Carl was secretly relieved. He'd managed to get rid of Devry, having him run up to Alden to re-interview a lady who gave terrible interviews, and now he was rid of Miller. He was going to interview Schultz's neighbors, but he was also going to look for Bob Czerczak again. Maybe have a chat with his neighbor. Before he'd come into the situation room, he had placed a call to

Czerczak's son in San Diego. The younger Czerczak was surprised and more than a little concerned to hear that his father had said he was traveling to see him. The old man wasn't in California. As a matter of fact, Bob Czerczak's son said, they hadn't spoken in weeks.

Twenty-Eight
September 9, 1980

After the fight with his father Mike drove around aimlessly for a half hour, trying to calm down. As his anger and frustration were starting to ebb, he realized how exhausted he was. It was too late to call anyone or knock on someone's door and he was considering finding a quiet place to park and sleep when he remembered he had a key for the service department door at the dealership where he worked. He pulled into the lot and parked his car towards the back. He climbed out, looked around and satisfied no one had seen him pull in, entered the back of the service department. He kicked off his boots and fell onto the couch in the customer waiting area. The next day was Saturday and the shop didn't open until nine a.m. He was sure he could be up and out before then.

After a fitful few hours of sleep he awoke at seven and went into the restroom to splash water on his face. He went to the Your Host Restaurant on the plaza and had breakfast. All the time he was considering what to do next. He needed to find a place to stay. Nick wasn't really an option since Nick's father was probably on the verge of kicking him to the curb. Eddie and Glenda? Not really. It was right around the corner from his father and besides that, the Kolbs had enough drama of their own going on. In any event, he would have to go to the house to pick up his clothes and the few possessions he considered essential. He knew his father usually worked the afternoon shift on Saturdays at the gas station so he had some time to kill until then if he wanted to avoid the old man.

He went to the library on Harlem and spent a few hours there reading magazines and looking at books about vintage cars. He went to the Thruway Mall and had lunch. Finally after 2 o'clock he made his way to his parent's house. His saw that his father's car was gone as he pulled up and parked in front of the house. He got out and walked up the front walk and rang the bell. His mother answered. Her eyes were red rimmed and her hair was a mess.

"Michael. What happened last night?" she asked.

"I need to get some stuff," was all he said as he brushed past her. She grabbed him by the sleeve. "Michael…"

He stopped and looked down at her. She looked more forlorn than he had ever seen her.

"Dad kicked me out," he said.

"I know, he told me that. But why? What happened?"

"I basically told him I was sick of his shit."

She let go of his sleeve and looked out the door. Mike started to climb the stairs. "He wasn't always like this," he heard her say. He went to his room and stuffed as many things into an old suitcase and a few bags he found and came back downstairs. His mother was still standing at the door, wringing a tissue in her hands.

"Where are you going?" she asked. Her voice was starting to tremble.

"I don't know yet." He opened the door but something made him stop. He looked at his mother. "I'll tell you when I get settled."

She looked at him and then looked away. She dabbed her eyes with the wadded up tissue.

"Mom, I can't live here anymore. Not with him."

She shook her head slowly.

"He's angry all the time," Mike went on. "And I'm sick of him taking it out on me."

"You don't understand." she said quietly.

"No, I understand it now. He's pissed off at the world like it did him wrong. Instead of doing something about it he just gets drunk and blames everybody else."

"He wasn't always like this," she said again.

"Maybe not, but he's like this now and I'm sick of it."

She looked at him full on. "You don't understand!" she said. "You don't know what it's like to sacrifice and keep a family together!"

Mike felt like he was on the verge of crying himself. "Maybe you're right," he said. "All I know is that I have to get out of this place. "And you should think about getting away from the asshole too!"

She shook her head again and started crying in full. Mike couldn't take any more, so he pushed the front door open and dragged his belongings to the car.

Twenty-Nine

June 21, 1988

It was still hot and humid when Carl rolled up to the front of 11 Clover Place. All this humidity and it still hadn't rained in weeks. His shirt was sticking to his back as he climbed out of the unmarked car. There were two cars in the driveway at number 11. He turned to look across the street at Bob Czerczak's house. It was dark and all the windows were closed. He'd get back to that later.

His first order of business was to knock on the door of the Schultz's former residence. The present owners were a couple in their thirties with a couple of kids. They had never met the Shultz's. The sale had been handled by the realtor. Carl got the name and number for the agent they had dealt with, thanked them and went to the house to the left of number 11.

There was a For Sale sign on the brown front lawn. As he got closer, he noticed that there were no curtains or blinds in the front window and after peering in, he realized that the house was deserted. He wrote the contact information for the realtor on the For Sale sign and made a note to see if they could run down the former occupants.

Next, the house to the right of number 11. After ringing the bell and knocking, the door was answered by a heavy set middle aged woman with her hair up in rollers. She said that she had lived there for twelve years and did in fact remember the Shultz's

"The wife was nice enough," she said. "Quiet little thing. But the husband? Not a very pleasant man. He used to yell at my kids for the littlest things..."

"Do you know where they moved to?"

She shook her head. "No, like I said, the wife was nice, but thanks to her asshole husband, pardon my French, we didn't really talk that often."

"There was a son? Michael?" Carl asked.

"Yeah, moody kid. I think he moved out a few years ago. Didn't see him around too often after that. The few times I did see him he was getting into it with his father."

"What do you mean?"

"They must have had some kind of falling out. The kid usually came around when the father was out. The few times they were there together you could tell there was no love lost." Carl wrote the name Michael down in his notebook and underlined it.

Carl realized he had left the picture of Jane Doe on his desk and silently cursed himself. He thanked the woman and walked back to his car. Another long look at Bob Czerczak's house as he hesitated by the driver's side door. "Fuck it," he said to himself. He walked across the street and up to the front door. He listened for a moment. The house was deathly quiet. He walked to the garage and peered in through the dirty window. "Son of a bitch!" Bob's car was gone. He turned around and saw the man he had spoken to the day before, pulling a garbage can to the curb. "Hey!" Carl called out.

The old man looked startled. He looked at Carl, who was now walking toward him and frowned. He was thin, almost to the point of being unhealthy. Carl saw that he had a slight tremor that he hadn't noticed the day before. Carl stopped a few feet away from the man, who had not moved and was gazing at Carl with a look of disdain.

"I don't suppose you've seen Mr. Czerczak, have you?" Carl was trying to hide his anger.

"Nope," was the only reply.

Carl shook his head. "You realize he's not in San Diego?"

"You don't say?"

The man's attitude was only making Carl angrier. He started to step closer but the guy looked like a stiff breeze would knock him over. "Look," he said. "His car's gone. Did you see him today?"

"Nope."

"You have no idea where he is?"

"I don't know. Is it a crime to leave your house?"

"No," Carl stared hard at the man. "But obstructing a police investigation is." Mr. Czerczak may be a witness to a homicide and I need to speak to him."

The old man looked suddenly concerned and his tremor grew slightly more animated. Carl broke off his stare and attempted a softer tone. "I don't know what you know, but the sooner I talk to Bob, the sooner we get this cleared up. If you know anything at all, now's the time to say it."

The old man looked down at the ground. "He didn't say where he was going," he said quietly.

"You saw him today?"

The man nodded. "He was home yesterday too, when you came by. After you left he came to the door and told me you were a PBA rep looking for a donation."

Carl laughed at that, despite himself. "And today?" he asked.

"I was watering the lawn and I saw him backing out of the garage. I flagged him down and asked him if he wanted a ride somewhere. He's really not supposed to drive, because of the stroke and all. He said he was fine though, and Bob can be stubborn as a mule. He said he was just running a few errands and then he left."

"What time was this?" Carl asked.

"About eight this morning. And he hasn't been back since."

Carl looked at his watch, it was after Seven PM. "Well shit," Carl said. Bob Czerczak was officially on the run.

"I don't understand," the old man said, his voice quivering slightly. "I hope he's not in trouble. Bob's a good man."

"I know," Carl said. "I just really need to talk to him."

Thirty

Nick had called Mike at 3:00 that afternoon and had asked him if he could help him with his car. The previous year, Mikes' boss at the dealership, Ken Rozek had left to open his own repair shop and offered Mike a job. Mike at first was hesitant until Ken offered him a lot more money than he would make in the foreseeable future at the dealership. Any other doubts he had about leaving the dealership were erased when the owner found out Mike was considering the offer. He blew his top and accused Mike of being "a disloyal little shit." It didn't take long for Rozek's Auto Repair to establish a loyal clientele and Mike didn't miss the bullshit that went along with working at the dealership.

Mike told Ken he would lock up after he finished a tune-up he was doing and waited for Nick. Nick finally showed up in a car that wasn't his at about 6:15.

Mike and Nick had been roommates for the past two and a half years. It turned out the only place they could afford was in the heart of Tiorunda. It was small and dingy but they were on their own and it suited their lifestyle. Nick had been drifting from job to job and was currently working at the print shop on George Urban Boulevard. Nick was still drinking heavily and now doing his fair share of coke. Mike would occasionally join Nick in his revelries, but found he was losing his taste for the lifestyle. He hated going to work hungover and didn't like the way cocaine made him feel. Nick never pressured him. He seemed to know when Mike needed to do his own thing. Also, to his credit, Nick never was late with his share of the rent. Mike knew that despite his spotty employment record, Nick made most of his money from working for Eddie Kolb.

Mike had tried to steer clear of Eddie, only going by the house when his curiosity about Glenda got the better of him. When he saw her she was either effusive or happy or seemed worn out and withdrawn. In either case, she always seemed to be under the influence of something.

Things with his parents were getting worse. He tried to time his visits to when his father would be out and wasn't always successful. When the old man was there it would always end up in a shouting match and Mike was reminded that he wasn't welcome. His mother always seemed sad and increasingly withdrawn.

"I thought we were working on your car?" Mike asked after Nick had pulled a strange car into the service bay.

"It's Eddie's," Nick replied. Mike noticed that Nick was avoiding making eye contact.

"What's wrong with it?"

Nick finally looked at him and said. "One of the lug nuts on the right rear tire is stuck. Can you get it off?"

Mike went to the switch and hoisted the car on the lift. He looked at the tire. "What's wrong with it?" When Nick didn't reply he turned to face him.

"I just need it off okay?"

"Why would you want to replace a perfectly good..." Mike stopped himself. Nick was staring at him somewhat irritated.

"Fuck, Nick," Mike said shaking his head.

"You said you didn't want to know about it," Nick said.

"I also said I didn't want to get involved, remember?"

"You're not. You're just changing a tire, grease monkey."

Mike walked over to where Nick was standing. "How much coke is in that tire Nicky?"

Nick smirked. "Now you're getting involved," he said.

Mike shook his head. He went over and picked up the pneumatic wrench and started to work on the lugs.

Thirty-One

After his conversation with Bob Czerczak's neighbor, Carl sat in his car and turned the air conditioner on full blast. He thought about going back to the station to pull records on the Shultz's, Bob Czerczak and the Kolbs to try to figure out what connection, if any, existed.

He was exhausted and in desperate need of a shower and a drink so he headed home.

The apartment was dark and quiet. After a shower he poured himself three fingers of bourbon and sat in his recliner. He picked up the remote for the TV and then set it down. His mind kept going back to the things he had learned as well as the new questions that had arisen the last few days. Before he had finished the whiskey he fell into a fitful sleep. He awoke in the dark after three a.m. and went to bed, setting the alarm for seven.

He was at his desk before eight, organizing his thoughts on a legal pad. Captain D'Agostino was already in his office with his door shut, engrossed in something on his desk. The rest of the squad room was empty at the moment and Carl was taking full advantage of the quiet. No sign of Devry yet. Carl wondered if Devry had shaken anything out of the old lady with the name Mary Schultz. If Jane Doe wasn't Mary Schultz they were back at square one. If it was Mary Schultz at the County Home then where was Arthur Shultz?

"Son of a bitch!" Carl said out loud. He got up from his desk, went to D'Agostino's door and knocked loudly.

"Come in," he heard D'Agostino call out.

Carl pushed the door open to find D'Agostino looking at him uneasily. "Carl? What's up?"

"We need to get a rush on the medical and dental records for Mary and Arthur Schultz."

"Okay," the captain said in a calm voice. "Why?"

Carl realized he was sweating and he probably looked a little crazed. "I'm going to chase down the lack of a forwarding address right now."

D'Agostino nodded uncertainty. "Ah, okay."

Carl shook his head. "The Shultz's fell off the map two years ago. I think we found Mary at the County Home. I have a hunch we may have found Arthur too."

Thirty-Two

MIKE WOKE TO the sound of the phone ringing in the kitchen. He looked at the clock on his nightstand, it was 12:18 a.m. He pulled himself out of bed and went into the kitchen.

"Hey" Nick said over the line when Mike picked up.

"Shit Nick, It's late. I have to be at work at seven."

"I'm in some shit Mike," Nick said. Mike could hear the concern in his voice. He was fully awake now.

"What's going on?"

"I'm at the holding center."

"What?"

There was a pause and then Nick started, "I got stopped coming back over the Peace Bridge form Canada."

"Holy shit Nick…"

"Yeah, well."

Mike thought for a moment and then asked the inevitable, "What do you want me to do?"

"They set a bail hearing for the morning and I have to get out of here."

"Did they say how much it could be?"

Nick sounded like he was on the verge of tears. "Ten grand, that's if they even grant it."

Mike wondered how much contraband they had found in Nick's

car but knew better than to ask. "Shit Nick, I don't have that kind of money laying around."

"I know," Nick said. "I've been trying to get a hold of Eddie. His fucked up old lady said he's not at home and when I called the bar they said he's not there."

Eddie had recently opened a bar at the corner of Genesee and Erb Street, a few blocks from the city line. It was formerly a neighborhood bar that he was trying to convert into a party spot with bands and DJs. The neighborhood was less than ideal for Eddie's plan and the business was faltering. To a point it didn't matter though, Eddie was using the business to sell drugs and launder money.

Mike closed his eyes and cursed silently. "Do you think he's at the bar?" he asked.

"He should be," Nick answered. "Mike, I'm sorry, but I don't know what else to do."

"I'll go look for him."

He hung up and went back to his room. He pulled on a pair of jeans and his work boots and went out into the steamy August night.

Ten minutes later he pulled into the parking lot of the furniture store that was a few doors down from the bar. Mike looked up and down the seemingly deserted street. It was a Thursday morning, the only hint of life was the dull thump of bass coming from the bar. Even though the bar was technically in Cheektowaga the area resembled the City of Buffalo's East Side more. It was lined with two story buildings built in the forties and fifties, small businesses on the lower floor, bars, bakeries, tailor shops with an apartment upstairs for the businesses' owners. Half of the businesses were shuttered now, a sign of the area's decline. Mike walked into the bar. There were only a few people in the place. The only one he recognized was Sheila the bartender, a girl who had been a year behind him at Maryvale High School. A Huey Lewis song was playing from the record player in the sound booth as Mike walked up to the bar. Sheila was engrossed in a conversation with a neighborhood guy who seemed to be trying to hit on her with little success. She took a bill off the bar and turned towards the cash register, finally seeing Mike. "Hey Mikey! How are you?" She put a coaster in front of him. He noticed her pupils were dilated and she was slurring her words. It was too bad, he thought. Sheila was a pretty girl, not terribly bright but a good person. Now she worked for Eddie Kolb and the effects were showing.

"Is Eddie here?" he asked.

"Um..." she hesitated, her eyes darting to the doorway to the back room, where the makeshift stage was.

Mike didn't wait. "Thanks," he said and went to the doorway. Eddie and Tony were seated at a table in the back room. There were several empty beer bottles and shot glasses between them. Tony saw Mike first and got Eddie's attention. Eddie looked up at Mike.

"Mr. Schultz," Eddie said. "What brings you to my establishment on this balmy evening?"

The song ended and there was a pause while another record dropped onto the turntable. "Nick's in trouble," Mike said.

Eddie nodded and then said, "I see. And what does that have to do with me?"

Mike shook his head. "Are we really going to do this?"

"Do what?" Eddie asked, the smile leaving his face. A heavy metal song started, filling the background with power chords, drums and a heavy bass.

"He got caught with your fucking drugs," Mike said over the music.

Tony started to stand up but Eddie put his hand on his arm and the big man sat back down. Eddie stood up himself then and turned to face Mike full on. "Nicky always said you thought you were above all this."

"What does that have to do with anything right now?" Mike asked. Eddie was a full four inches taller than Mike, but Mike met his gaze full on.

"What it means, my young friend, is that now is not a good time for you to get involved. Nick knew the risks and the consequences."

The men's room door opened and a man Mike had seen at the bar once or twice walked over to where they were standing.

"What does that mean?" Mike asked.

"Something I learned in Vietnam. If things get shitty, you do what you have to do to survive. But the last thing you do is rat out your brothers."

Mike shook his head. "Your brothers? You're a fucking drug dealer," he said, his voice rising.

"Easy kid," the stranger said. He was big like Tony and had an anchor tattoo on his forearm.

Mike glanced at him dismissively and then looked back at Eddie. Mike could see that Eddie was getting angry, but he didn't care. "Who the fuck do you think you are?" he asked. "You piss all over the people who work for you and don't even get me started on how you treat your wife."

A quick, mirthless smile flashed Eddie's face. "Why you sanctimonious little prick."

"Fuck you Eddie," Mike said peevishly.

A flash of pain on the right side of his head. The stranger had cold cocked him. Mike was staggered but stayed on his feet. He turned to face the stranger who was cocking his fist for another punch. Before Mike reset his feet to defend himself Eddie grabbed him by the shoulders and pushed him face first into the wall. Tony had silently got to his feet and was now helping Eddie hold Mike against the wall. Sheila entered the room, took in what was happening and stood there with her mouth hanging open.

"Get back to the fucking bar," Eddie grunted. She closed her mouth, looked at them for another second and then left.

Eddie was right in Mike's ear. "Like I said, asshole," he hissed. "Now is not an ideal time to concern yourself with things that don't concern you." He drove his elbow into the back of Mike's neck for emphasis. "That would include, me, my business and especially..." another shove into the back of Mike's neck, "my wife." He let up and Tony and the stranger immediately were on either side seizing Mike by the arms. "Get him out of here," Eddie ordered. "Take him out the side door."

Mike was dragged by his arms and the scruff of his neck to the fire exit on the side of the back room. The stranger kicked the door open; he was roughly pushed out. He foot missed the step and he fell face first into the filthy, weed strewn alley. He broke his fall with his hands and a stab of pain immediately stung his right palm. He rolled over and looked at his hand. There was a piece of broken bottle sticking out of it. He gingerly removed it with his other hand and the blood started to flow from the cut. He looked up at the two men in the doorway. Tony's usual stoic countenance had been replaced by something Mike had never seen before. He looked sad and worried. The stranger on the other hand was grinning like an idiot. "Have a nice night now, you hear?" he said and then slammed the door.

THIRTY-THREE

JUNE 22, 1988

CARL WAS WAITING impatiently in the situation room. After weeks of spinning his wheels with the investigation he finally felt like progress was being made. Now he had to wait for other members of the task force to finish their parts and prove his theory right.

Devry had come into the station shortly after 8:00 a.m. and reported that his previous night's visit with their Jane Doe in the County Hospital had proved more or less fruitless. When he asked her if her name was Mary Schultz she didn't respond, only staring back blankly at him. Devry did say she had a slight reaction to the name Michael but not enough to convince him. Carl and D'Agostino filled him in on the latest developments and Devry said he would make a few calls regarding a forwarding address for the Shultz's after the sale of their home. Bill Miller was still trying to run down the Schultzes medical and dental records and had disappeared from his desk at about 8:30.

It was going on ten o'clock and Carl had done everything he could think of to update the case file and the information on the bulletin board. He was on his fourth cup of coffee and was starting to feel the jitters. Mazerowski, one of the desk Sergeants, stuck his head into the room and said, "Carl, Miller is on line three."

"Thanks Maz," Carl said. He walked over to the phone, picked up the receiver and punched the line. "Miller! Where are you?"

"At the Medical Examiners."

"What are you doing there?"

"I found the Shultz's dental records like you told me to. It wasn't easy. Their dentist retired last year and the practice was taken over by some new guy."

"Why didn't you call me?" Carl asked.

"The prissy little bitch at the dentist's office wouldn't let me use her phone. I figured I'd call from here. Anyway turns out you were probably right."

Carl felt his pulse quicken. "Right about what?" he asked.

He heard Miller flipping a page in his notebook. "A preliminary examination of the x-rays are almost definitely a match with the deceased," Miller read.

"You mean?"

"Yep," Miller said. "Our stiff is the late Arthur P. Schultz."

"Son of a bitch…"

Carl hung up and walked over to the board. He wrote the name Arthur Shultz on the picture the crime scene techs had taken of the body in the freezer. He was wondering how and why no one had noticed that Arthur Shultz's life had been taken and his body had been discarded so casually. Jane Doe was almost certainly Mary Shultz, the deceased's wife. Who knew what was going through the crazy old bat's mind? And if the ME's timeline was right, how did Arthur complete the sale of his house after he was presumably dead?

Devry walked in, followed by D'Agostino. They both looked at the board and then at Carl who nodded at them.

"Miller found dental records and we have a match," Carl said.

"Well you're going to want to see this then," Devry said. He placed a small stack of photo copies on the table and turned them towards Carl.

"What am I looking at?" Carl asked, taking his reading glasses out of his shirt pocket.

"I have a friend in the Postmaster's office" Devry said. "I was able to expedite the information on where the Shultz's mail went after they sold the house on Clover."

Carl scanned the pages. For a year after the sale of their house in '86, the Schultz's mail was delivered to a PO box at the post office on Genesee Street. Last year though, the rental was terminated and what little mail they received went to the Dead Letter Office. Carl thought for a moment and asked, "But if Arthur is already dead and the wife is, well, not well, who was picking up their mail."

"Go to the last page," Devry answered.

Carl flipped to the last page. It was a copy of the initial rental agreement for the box. The signature at the bottom clearly read: *Michael A. Schultz.*

CARL COULD FEEL the adrenaline kick in. Captain D'Agostino had said something about a warrant, but Carl insisted they pick Michael Schultz up for questioning sooner rather than later. D'Agostino relented and sent Carl, Bill Miller and a couple of uniformed officers to the address Schultz had listed with the post office in Tiorunda. They sped up to the front of the unit and Carl was out of the car before Miller had it in park.

"Jesus, Carl," Miller protested.

"C'mon," Carl grunted. He hurried to the front of the unit with the others in tow and rapped on the door. A moment later a middle-aged black woman holding a baby opened the door. She looked alarmed as she saw the four men standing in front of her.

"We're looking for Michael Schultz," Carl said. He knew though, that something was off.

She shook her head nervously and the baby started to fuss. "Nobody here by that name," she said.

Carl took a breath and tried to rein in his anxiety. "Do you live here ma'am?"

Another head shake, "No, this is my daughter's apartment. I'm watching my grandson while she's at work."

"How long has your daughter lived here?"

She thought for a moment and said, "A little over a year?"

Carl cursed under his breath. Miller cleared his throat and spoke up. "Is there a rental office in the complex?"

"No," the woman said. "She sends the rent to an address in the city." The baby started to cry then. "And no, I don't know the address," she added slightly aggravated.

Carl was fighting the urge to push past the woman and toss the apartment to find a phone number or address for the landlord. He felt Miller's hand on his arm. "Sorry to disturb you ma'am," Miller said calmly. The woman closed the door. Carl was still facing the doorway, the adrenaline rush now subsiding. "We can get the landlord's info at the station Carl," Miller said. "God knows we have enough paperwork on the place."

Carl turned and started walking back towards the car with a knot forming in his stomach. Another person of interest had vanished. He could feel in the pit of his stomach that Mike Schultz, just like Bob Czerczak, had something to hide, maybe more so. He wondered how hard Schultz had worked to cover his tracks.

Thirty-Four

It wasn't until two days later that Mike heard from Nick. Nick had called him at lunchtime at the shop and Mike asked his boss if he could cut for an hour or two. He assured Ken that he would stay late and finish the car he was working on. A half hour later he pulled up in front of the Federal Court House on Niagara Square. Nick was waiting, smoking a cigarette in the same clothes Mike had seen him in two days earlier.

Nick climbed in silently and Mike pulled away from the curb, rounding the circle and turning right on Genesee. "You made bail?" he asked.

"My dad came up with the bond," Nick answered.

"Where is he?"

Nick looked out the side window and answered, "He left. He said 'that was it, we're done,' and he left."

Mike let the words hang there for a moment. "Did they set a trial date?" he finally asked.

"Not yet. They assigned a public defender. Asshole kept forgetting my name. He said he's going to be in touch."

"This is bad, Nick."

"No shit," Nick snapped.

A strained silence fell over the car for the next few blocks. Mike finally cleared his throat and asked, "Did they offer any kind of deal?"

Nick looked at Mike. His eyes were bloodshot and he looked beaten down. "It came up."

"And?"

"Nothing."

"Fucking Eddie," Mike said.

"I know. He said he'd take care of things if they went to shit."

Mike thought about his run in with Eddie and his friends the other night. "What are you going to do?" he asked.

"I don't know yet," Nick responded looking back out the side window. "I gotta do something though or I'm fucked.

THREE DAYS WENT by. Nick's lawyer called that Monday and said the preliminary hearing was set for August 21st. Again, he told Nick he could make things better by offering the DEA some names and Nick said he would think about it. He went back to work on the midnight shift at the print shop, telling his supervisor that his father had had a heart attack and apologizing for missing work without calling in. Mike went back to work at the shop and would come home to an empty apartment in the afternoon. That Thursday it was the same. It was after nine p.m. and there was no sign of Nick. Mike was about to go to bed when he realized that the kitchen garbage was starting to smell and decided to take it out to the dumpster. On his way back, the door to the unit two doors down from his opened. It was a man he only knew as "Lapper," a member of the Chosen Few Motorcycle Club. Lapper stepped out and looked at him. He was heavy-set and had a scraggly beard, his sleeveless shirt exposed two thick arms covered with tattoos.

"You're Mike, right?" Lapper asked.

"Yeah."

"Have you seen your roommate?"

"Um' no, he's not home right now."

Lapper scratched under his chin and pursed his lips.

"Why do you ask," Mike wondered.

"He knocked on my door tonight. He looked kinda… fucked up."

"Why? What did he want?" Mike asked.

Lapper looked right at him. "He said he wanted to buy a piece."

Fuck, Mike thought. Nick wanted a gun. Nothing about that felt right.

"Even if I had one to sell him," Lapper continued, "I wouldn't considering his state of mind."

Mike considered that for a moment and then said, "Thanks."

Lapper went back inside his apartment, closing the door behind him. Mike stood where he was for a few moments, his mind racing. The last few days Nick had been trying to act cool, but Mike could tell that Nick's worst urges were rising to the surface. He went back to his apartment, pulled on a pair of jeans and grabbed the car keys.

Ten minutes later he parked down the street from Eddie's bar. As he approached he noticed the light that illuminated the sign over the door was out, same with the neon beer signs in the front window. The next thing that caught his eye was the sedan parked directly in front of the bar with Ontario plates. He was considering turning around and heading home when he spotted Nick's Pontiac further down the block. "Shit," he said under his breath. He walked closer to the bar. There was no one in the sedan in front. He was passing the narrow alley between the bar and the building next door and thought he saw something in the dim light. He stepped into the alley and as his eyes adjusted to the gloom he saw that he had been right. There was a person lying in just about the same spot where he had landed the week before.

"No, no, no," he whispered to himself as he walked quietly along the wall towards the shape.

The side door to the bar was open, there was no music playing tonight but he could hear voices, speaking in a muffled conversation. He walked into the alley as far as he thought reasonable, his boots crunching on the gravel and a few bits of broken glass. He was about ten feet from the person in the alley when he breathed a sigh of relief. There was enough light coming from the side door to reveal that it wasn't Nick lying in the alley; it was the man who had sucker punched and then ejected Mike the previous week. His relief was tempered though when he got a good look at the man. He had a large gash on his forehead and he was bleeding profusely from his mouth, he had definitely had some teeth knocked out. Worse though, was the fact that the man wasn't moving, he showed no outward signs of life. He thought about Nick and then about his own self-preservation. He turned to head back down the alley. He had to call the cops. Nick would be better off in jail than ending up dead or half dead in an alley.

"Hey!" He heard a voice from behind him. He turned briefly and saw that someone had emerged from the side door of the bar, a silhouette looking in his direction. He turned again and started towards the street, but there was another silhouette blocking his path. A looming figure with a gun in his right hand.

Mike was escorted in through the side door. The man on the ground still hadn't moved. His eyes swept the room. Eddie was standing against the far wall. He was red-faced and perspiring. There was a man standing in front of Eddie, who looked Asian or mixed-race at least. He was about five foot ten and lean, in a dress shirt and slacks. There was a black man standing next to him, holding an automatic pistol at his side with his finger on the trigger guard. The two men who had brought Mike into the bar were standing slightly behind him and Mike couldn't see what they looked like. The only thing he noticed was that one of them was enormous, at least six five. Finally he saw Nick, seated on a wooden chair in the corner. He was barely conscious and his face was a bloody mess. There was no sign of Tony or anyone else in the bar.

The Asian man looked at Mike and then the two men behind him. "Who the fuck is this?" he asked.

The giant grabbed Mike by the scruff of the neck and growled, "Who the fuck are you?"

Mike winced from the pain and couldn't have spoken at that moment even if he wanted to.

"That's his girlfriend," Eddie said, gesturing towards Nick.

The giant pushed Mike in Nick's direction. Mike almost fell on his face but regained his balance and looked down at his friend. Nick looked up through swollen eyes and then coughed up a little blood.

"Is he one of your employees as well?" he heard the Asian man ask.

"Nah," Eddie said. "He used to be 'til he found Jesus." Mike looked over at Eddie who shot him a dirty look and then looked back at his interrogator.

The room was quiet for a moment. The Asian man looked around and then back at Eddie. "Where were we?"

"The DEA has your product man," Eddie said.

"I know that, Edward," the man said.

Eddie continued, "And I never received it thanks to the kid over there, therefore; I couldn't sell it. Therefore, I don't have the money."

"Hmm," the Asian man muttered. He walked over to Nick and put his hand on his shoulder. Nick barely reacted. His head bobbed up and down. The man put his hand under his chin and lifted

Nick's face. "Eddie, is this how you treat all your employees?"

"The ones who fuck up and then come back at me because they can't accept the fact that they fucked up."

The man let Nick's chin fall back to his chest. "That's our problem Eddie," he said as he wiped his hand off on Nick's shirt. "Your story has a few holes in it."

"What...what are you talking about?" Eddie answered flatly.

He stepped towards Eddie. As he did, he produced a butterfly knife from his pocket and flipped it open skillfully. Eddie's eyes shot around the room, probably searching for an exit. The other three men were casually inching in his direction.

"Your friend, Tony?" the man said. "We had an interesting conversation in his mother's garage. Tony told us, and I don't know why he would lie given how persuasive we were being, that you tipped off the customs people at the Peace Bridge because you were going to use that as an excuse to end our arrangement."

"Bullshit!" Eddie yelled.

"Eddie!" the man roared back. "Stop! You're only embarrassing yourself now. We know you already have another supplier here in the States. Tony gave it all up."

Eddie's mouth opened and nothing came out. He took a step away from the wall and the man with the pistol immediately pointed it at Eddie's head. The giant and the fourth man, who was as tall as Eddie himself, approached Eddie on either side.

"What do you want Alex?" Eddie asked the Asian man.

Alex shrugged. "Just the 100K you screwed me out of," he replied.

Eddie laughed nervously and shook his head. "Alex I don't have it," he said.

"I know," Alex said. He nodded at the giant who lunged forward with speed that belied his size and punched Eddie in the stomach.

Eddie doubled over and the giant and his partner grabbed Eddie by the arms and threw him back up against the wall.

With their attention focused on Eddie, Mike briefly considered bolting for the front door, which he assumed was locked. He looked down at Nick and realized that they wouldn't make it three steps before they were stopped.

"Twenty-four hours, Edward," Alex said, flipping the knife open and closed. The man holding Eddie's right arm pinned it up against the wall and then Alex walked up, pinned Eddie's wrist down and deftly cut off Eddie's pinkie finger.

Eddie grunted and then howled in pain. Blood was spurting out and dripping down the dirty wall. He stopped screaming and went back to grunting. Alex took out a handkerchief and wiped the blood off the blade of his knife. He put the knife back into his pocket and said, "Twenty-four hours, Edward. I won't be back to collect. I'm slightly concerned about crossing the border now, thanks to you. I have associates on this side though who will by to collect and if they don't have it they will take more than your little finger next time." The two goons let up their grip on Eddie doubled over, clutching his injured hand. "And if we run out of parts to take from you we'll start on your wife," Alex finished.

"What about these two?" the man with the gun asked. Mike realized the man was looking at Nick and him.

Alex paused for a moment and then looked at Mike and Nick as if he had just remembered they were still there. "What about them?" he asked.

"What do you want to do with them?"

Alex shrugged and then said, "Nothing. I think this was a teachable moment for all involved." He walked towards the front door with the other three in tow. He unlocked it and turned around. "Eddie," he said. "You might want to send Tony's mother a nice card. He won't be working on her car anymore." With that Alex and his men walked out the front door.

Mike was frozen. He looked at Eddie who was down on his knees clutching his injured hand. Eddie finally looked up. "What?" Eddie grunted.

Mike finally snapped out of his fog. He pulled Nick out of his seat and with one of Nick's arms over his shoulder made his way to the front door.

THIRTY-FIVE
JUNE 23, 1988

THE DAY BEFORE, a frustrated Carl Wisneiwski had returned to the station with Bill Miller and met with Captain D'Agostino to discuss their next steps. Mike Shultz's records with the New York State DMV had been accessed and the address in Tiorunda was still listed as his place of residence. With nothing else to do for the day, D'Agostino sent the detectives home with the plan to reconvene the next morning and explore other avenues.

Carl went home to his apartment on French Avenue. The air was stuffy when he entered. He turned the air conditioner up and stripped off his shirt. Then he went to the kitchen and took the bottle of bourbon out of the cupboard and poured a few ounces into a glass. He went back to the dining area and found the sport coat he had thrown over a chair and retrieved his notebook. He sat down at the table, lit a cigarette and opened the notebook.

His eyes were scanning the pages, but nothing was registering. He pushed the notebook away, sat back in his chair and took a healthy drink.

The next morning the team convened in the situation room just after eight. Jeff Devry had come up with a list of agencies that might have records for Mike Schultz. The list was divided among the detectives and D'Agostino and the phone calls began. A half hour later Bill Miller was standing over Carl's Desk with his notebook in his hand.

"Want to take a ride?" Miller asked.

Carl looked up and took his reading glasses off. "What do you have?" he asked.

"I just got off the phone with the State Department of Taxation and Finance. Before you get too excited they had nothing on Schultz for the last two years."

"But?" Carl prompted.

"He was working at a garage on Union Road as recently as '85."

Carl sat back and thought. He'd been getting the run around from the Social Security Department for the last twenty minutes and was feeling restless. He stood up and took his sport coat off the back of his chair. "Well, that's something," he said. "Let's see what Devry is up to."

Devry was, in fact, on the phone in the situation room, currently on hold with the IRS. Carl told him what Miller had discovered and then brought D'Agostino up to speed and left the station.

They pulled into the lot at Rozek's Automotive just after nine. There wasn't a place to park. The small lot was full of cars either waiting to be serviced or waiting to be picked up by their owners. All three bay doors were open and occupied by cars, one of them up on a lift. They walked into an airless office/customer waiting area and found it empty. Carl led the way through the side door into the first service bay. A boom box perched on a tool box was blasting a Rolling Stones song from the previous decade. The hood of the car was up and Carl walked around to the front of the car where he found a young man in his early twenties putting a distributor cap back on. The kid noticed Carl and almost hit his head on the hood when he straightened up. It wasn't Mike Shultz, that would have been too easy.

"Do you know a Michael Shultz?" Carl asked.

"Who?" the kid asked straining to hear over the music and the din coming from the next bay.

Miller said something inaudible, walked back over to the boom box and turned the volume down.

"Hey!" came a voice from the far bay. A tall man in his thirties in filthy overalls looked in their direction and frowned. The mechanic in the middle bay had stopped what he was doing and was now also looking in their direction.

Carl held up his badge and said, "We're trying to locate Michael Schultz."

"What'd he do?" the man in the middle bay asked.

"Never mind that, Skip," the man from the far bay said. He walked over to the first bay and stood in front of Carl. "I'm Ken Rozek, the owner. Why don't we step outside?" He looked from one of his employees to the other and added, "You two get back to work."

"What's this about?" Rozek asked once they were out of the garage. It was mid-morning but the sun was already beating down.

"I'm afraid I can't get into that," Carl answered. "Do you know Michael Schultz?"

"He used to work here."

"Used to?" Miller asked.

"Yeah he quit about three years ago."

"Do you know where he's working now?" Carl asked.

Rozek shook his head. "No. The thing is he didn't quit, he just stopped showing up."

"Any ideas why?"

"Nope, none. Actually that was kinda out of character for Mike. He was a good employee, pretty reliable and a good mechanic."

Carl considered for a moment; was this another dead end? Then a thought occurred to him. "Did he ever talk about his family?"

Rozek wiped some sweat from his forehead with a dirty rag and answered, "I know his old man was a prick. That's about it."

"Did he have any friends?"

"Not that…" Rozek stopped himself. "Wait, there was this one kid who used to come in and have Mike work on his car. Sketchy little bastard."

"You know his name?"

"Nicholas Arnetto."

Carl looked at Rozek and took out his notebook. "You came up with that in a hurry."

"Oh, I remember him," Rozek said. "He still owes the shop two hundred and forty bucks."

Thirty-Six

August 17, 1984

The previous night, Mike had loaded Nick into his car and sped over to nearby St. Joseph's Hospital on Harlem Road. On the way there, Nick had come to long enough to ask, "What happened?"

"Fucking Eddie set you up man," Mike responded.

"What?"

"He used you Nick. He sacrificed you to get out of dealing with that crazy Canadian."

"Alex?"

"Yeah," Mike nodded. "Fucking psychopath."

Nick's head bobbed up and down and he went under again.

Mike had to practically carry Nick into the emergency room. There were few people sitting on the hard plastic chairs in the waiting area. He walked Nick up to the admissions desk and a young nurse looked up at them. At first she seemed blasé, but after she got a good look at Nick she picked up the phone on her desk and punched in a number.

"I need a gurney at the front desk stat," she said firmly. She pulled a clipboard in front of her and asked, "Name?"

Nick didn't respond. He was looking in her direction with unfocused eyes.

"His name is Nicholas Arnetto," Mike answered. Two orderlies pushed their way through the double doors off to the side and wheeled a gurney in their direction. The nurse wrote down his name and looked at Mike. "What happened to him?"

Mike had no inclination to become further involved at the moment. He decided to start lying. "I don't know, he showed up at home like this."

The orderlies helped Nick onto the gurney. The nurse stood up and looked at Mike. "What is your name?"

"I'm his cousin. My name is Larry Arnetto."

"Did you contact the police, Larry?"

"Um no..." Mike replied.

She frowned and wrote something down on the clipboard. "Alright, have a seat," she said. "I have a few more questions for you." She turned and followed the orderlies and Nick through the double doors. Mike didn't hesitate. There was nothing he could do to help Nick now. He quickly walked back out the exit into the steamy night air.

Mike couldn't sleep that night. Nick was truly screwed now. He had a court date coming up and Eddie had not only set him up and cut him loose, but now was in a world of shit himself. What options did Eddie have? He had tried to screw over a truly dangerous organization and now everyone around him was going to have to deal with the fallout.

He thought about Glenda. What shitty decisions had she made to end up with a guy like Eddie? And why did she stay with him? The drugs? The liquor? Mike knew that she needed the kind of help that someone like Eddie Kolb would never be able to give her.

HE WENT TO work in the morning but couldn't seem to focus on anything. Just after lunch he told Ken, his boss, that he didn't feel good and went home. He checked the answering machine, there were no calls. He wondered about Nick. Was he alright? Was he

in custody? He called the hospital and was told that only imme-
diate family could be given any information regarding a patient.

Afternoon turned into evening. It was dusk and Mike was anxious and restless. He remembered that Eddie had a deadline that
was almost up. He grabbed his keys and headed out to his car.
The sun was sinking over the Thruway as he arrived at the end of
his old street and turned right onto Pinehurst. He drove slowly
past the Kolb's house with his heart beating quickly. No lights on
and no sign of Eddie's Dodge. He pulled to the side just past the
house and climbed out of the car. A light rain had started to fall.
He slowly walked up to the edge of the driveway. The house was
deathly quiet, the only sound was the hiss of tires on wet pavement
of the Interstate forty yards away. He slowly walked up the driveway, listening for any sound coming out of the house.

When he turned the corner at the back of the house he saw the
metal storm door hanging open. Shit, he thought. He walked up
the steps and into the open door.

She was sitting in the gloom at the kitchen table, smoking a cigarette with a glass of clear liquid in front of her. It took a moment
but she looked up at him. Her lower lip was swollen and her eyes
were red.

"Where is he?" Mike asked.

"He left," she replied. She looked at him and took a drag on the
cigarette. After she exhaled a plume of smoke she asked, "What
happened last night?"

Mike shut the wooden exterior door, walked over to the table
and sat down. "He didn't tell you?"

"No," she said, grinding the cigarette into a half full metal ashtray on the table. "He came crashing in this morning, his hand all
fucked up. He said he had to go and I asked him where. He said it
was better if I didn't know. I asked him how long he'd be gone for

and he said he didn't know. He was different, scared I think. I've never seen him like that." She looked back up at Mike expectantly.

Mike told her what had happened at the bar the previous evening. She listened intently, taking another cigarette out of the pack but not lighting it. He stopped right before the part about Alex threatening her too.

When he finished they sat quietly for a few minutes. She took a drink and finally lit the cigarette. After she exhaled she said, "I knew it was bad this time. He didn't even take the car. He stuck it in the garage and came back to get his bag. I asked him what was going on and he just went for the door. I grabbed his arm and that's when he did this," she said pointing to her lip.

"It's bad," Mike said quietly. She looked at him again. "I think you might be in trouble," he added.

"What do you mean?"

Mike shook his head and finished the story, complete with all the threats that Alex had made. Her brow furrowed and she looked confused.

"Glenda, this guy is a fucking psychopath. Is there anywhere you can go?"

She shook her head. "The only family I have around is my dad and he..." her voice trailed off.

Another silence fell over the room. "Alright," Mike said then. "You can come to my place."

"No," she said with another head shake. "What if Eddie comes back?"

Mike sincerely doubted that Eddie was coming back but he didn't want to say it and risk upsetting her further. Then he wondered if the cops were going to be at his place in the near future asking questions about Nick. He felt lost in the hopelessness of it all.

"Will you stay with me tonight?" He looked up at her after she said that. Her eyes were shining, hopeful.

"Yes," he said immediately.

"I'm tired," she said. She drained the glass and stamped out the cigarette. She stood up and looked down at him. "Thank you, Michael." She turned and left the room.

Mike sat still for a moment. He was exhausted as well. He finally stood up and made sure the doors were locked. After he locked the back door in the kitchen he had a thought and searched the drawers until he found a knife. The house was quiet again. He went upstairs to use the bathroom and splash cold water on his face. Out in the hallway he peered in as he passed Glenda's open bedroom door. She was curled up motionless on the bed. He wasn't sure if she was asleep so he quietly said, "I'll be downstairs on the couch."

'No," she said and rolled over to look at him in the near darkness. "Will you stay here with me?"

He walked over to the bed, placed the knife on the nightstand and pulled off his boots. His head was spinning from exhaustion. He laid down on the bed and put his head on the pillow next to her. Glenda pulled herself over to him and curled up with an arm over his chest. Mike realized that she knew Eddie was never coming back.

THIRTY-SEVEN
July 1, 1988

W<small>HEN NONE OF</small> the other government agencies they had reached out to could provide any current information on Mike Schultz, the task force decided to track down Nick Arnetto. He was easy to find. He currently resided at Attica State Prison, serving a five to ten year sentence for armed robbery. It took almost a week, but the trip was arranged for Carl and Devry to make the fifty minute drive to interview Arnetto.

Carl had read Nick Arnetto's file. He'd served six months on a Federal drug charge until he decided to flip on a Toronto dealer named Alex Chu. Nothing came of it as Chu had disappeared when the RCMP went to arrest him and turn him over to the Americans. Arnetto couldn't seem to stay out of trouble though. He had been arrested for aggravated assault once and was on probation when he was identified on a security camera holding up a convenience store on Niagara Street in the city. The judge took one look at his sheet and sent him to Attica.

They were almost in Bennington NY, speeding down Route 354. The sun was beating down on the blacktop as Carl, in the passenger seat, thumbed through the file folder.

"Ya ever been there?" Miller asked.

"Where?"

"Attica?"

"Nope," Carl said, taking his reading glasses off. "I knew a guy who died in the riots though."

"Shit. A CO?"

"No," Carl answered. "Guy by the name of Lenny Petrovic. Big dumb fucker. My second year on the job me and a couple of other guys go to serve a warrant on this guy Petrovic. Some aggravated assault beef. Anyway, he resists. Actually popped me in the eye. So we beat the shit out of him and bring him in. He gets sent up for a nickel and a month later the riot starts."

"That was '72?" Miller asked.

"'71." Carl corrected him. "Poor bastard wasn't even one of the rioters. A case of 'wrong time, wrong place.' He got shot when the Staties stormed the yard."

"Shit," Miller added.

A short time later they pulled into the parking area in front of the penitentiary.

Attica State Prison had been constructed in the 1930s. The gray walls looming above them resembled a medieval fortress. Entering the visitor's entrance, they found the inside was just as grim. They checked their weapons at the visitor's check in desk and were escorted to an interview room.

They waited for almost thirty minutes. Carl was getting antsy. He opened the door and approached the Sergeant at the desk in the corridor. "Any word on where my interview is?"

"Oh yeah, sorry Detective," the Sergeant said looking up. "Turns out he was put in solitary last night. I just got the paperwork."

"Solitary?" Carl asked.

The Sergeant shook his head. "Little Nicky likes to fight. He should be down in a couple of minutes."

Carl went back to the interview room and updated Miller. A few minutes later, Nick Arnetto was led into the room by two COs.

They attached his handcuffs to a metal ring on the table. Carl looked at Arnetto. He looked different than the mug shot Carl had seen, older, thinner. His hair was cut short and a scar was visible running from his forehead up though his scalp. He looked from Carl to Miller and back to Carl again. There was something feral about his mannerisms, Carl wondered if that was a result of being in this place.

"What's this about?" Arnetto asked.

Carl sat down across from Arnetto and took out a picture of Mike Schultz that they had copied and enlarged from a High School yearbook. He turned it and pushed it in front of Arnetto. "We're looking for your ex-roommate," he said.

Arnetto barely glanced down at the photo. He looked at Carl and said, "Mikey? I couldn't tell you where he is. Haven't seen him in years."

"You guys were tight though, right?" Miller said from off to the side.

Arnetto tried to sit back but the chains stopped him before he could fully recline. "I knew him."

"You lived together," Carl interjected. "You grew up in the same neighborhood."

Arnetto shrugged. "So?" he said. "That was a long time ago. He went his way and I went…" he looked around the room and raised his cuffed hands as far as he could. "And I went mine."

Carl frowned. "So you haven't been in touch with Mike Schultz since you've been inside?"

Arnetto said nothing. He seemed to be considering something.

"What?" Carl asked, growing impatient.

"Hypothetically," Arnetto started. "Say I had something to tell you."

"Here we go," Miller moaned.

Carl shook his head and took the photo back, placing in the file folder. "That ship has sailed, Junior," he said.

Arnetto sat back from the table. "Are you sure?"

Carl stood up and looked down at Arnetto. "You're a three time loser son. I doubt anything you tell me would be out of your interest in the public good."

Arnetto sat back again. "Well fuck off then, officer."

"I'll do that, asshole," Carl replied. "I'll do that while I'm sitting in my air conditioned apartment tonight and you're here with somebody's dick in your ass."

Arentto's face turned red and then he screamed, "Fuck you, Pig!"

The door to the corridor swung open immediately and one of the COs stepped in. "Everything alright?" he asked while staring at Arnetto.

"Yeah, we're done here," Carl said. He gathered up the picture and put it back in the file. Arnetto slumped back in his chair and looked up at Carl. "Let's go," Carl said to Miller.

Out in the corridor Miller asked, "What if he had something to give us? Shouldn't we at least give him a listen?"

Carl shook his head. "You heard him, if he had anything he's not going to give it up unless we give him something in return, which we can't."

"We could, um...stretch the truth," Miller offered.

Carl looked at Miller and slowed his pace. "That shitbird has nothing to lose. We start dicking around with him all we're doing is wasting more time," he said. "Besides, I have another idea."

A few minutes later they were at the visitor's check desk. With the Sergeant's approval they were scanning the sign in log books going back the last year. Every visitor had to present a photo ID and sign in to visit an inmate.

"Do you really think Schultz came out here to see him?" Miller asked. They'd been at it for over a half hour.

"That's what I'm hoping," Carl responded. He was thumbing through a binder labeled *March '88*. "Miller, look at this," Carl said suddenly. Miller stood up and stepped over to Carl and looked at the log book. Carl's thick finger pointing at a name on the list.

"Michael Kohler?" Miller asked

Carl opened his file folder again and took out a piece of paper. Miller recognized it as the PO Box rental agreement that Schultz had signed for his parents' mail after the sale of the house on Clover Place. The signatures were almost identical.

"Holy shit," Miller said.

"Yeah and not only that," Carl said standing up. "Kohler was Mary Shultz's maiden name.

Thirty-Eight

They finally came two nights later. Mike had agreed to stay with Glenda for a few days until they were sure she was safe. He had only returned to his apartment to get a few things and there had been no sign of Nick. He was either still in the hospital or maybe in custody. There was no way to be sure. On the 20th Mike had just gotten out of the shower after work when he heard voices downstairs. He pulled on his clothes and went to the stairs.

"Where is he?" he heard a strange man's voice ask.

"I don't know!" he heard Glenda respond.

As he came down the stairs he saw two men in the living room. The front door was open and it looked like they had pushed their way in. One of the men saw movement on the stairs and spun and glared at Mike. "Who the fuck are you?" he asked. He was wearing a button down shirt open over a t-shirt. Mike saw the gun tucked into his belt.

"He's just a friend," Glenda said.

The other man was wearing a black t-shirt stretched tight over his bulging arms and chest. He looked at Mike and said, "Come down here where we can see you, friend."

Mike complied and walked over to stand next to Glenda. She was trembling but otherwise seemed to be holding it together. "He took his shit and left two days ago," she offered.

Black t-shirt looked around the room. "That's no good," he said. "Your old man screwed the boss over pretty good and the boss needs something to…" he trailed off.

"Make it right," the man with the gun offered.

"Yeah, that's it," T-shirt agreed.

Glenda's trembling intensified and Mike fought off the urge to put his arms around her. The fewer movements the better, he thought.

A shadow filled the front door. The man with the gun turned quickly, pulled back the shirt and put his hand on the butt of the gun.

"Easy partner," the man in the doorway said. It was Bob, the retired cop, standing with his palms up. "I come in peace."

"And who the fuck are you?" T-shirt asked.

"Just a neighbor," Bob answered.

"A fucking nosy neighbor," the man with the gun said.

Bob took a tentative step in and cleared his throat. "True, I was just looking for young Michael here and I wandered in on your conversation."

"And you should wander the fuck back out," T-shirt said.

"I think I could help," Bob replied.

"How's that?"

"Eddie's gone," Bob went on. "We all know that." He paused and let the words sink in. "Maybe we could negotiate something. Something to compensate you and your employer for the trouble that Eddie caused.

The two thugs were staring at Bob. Bob looked around the room and then at Glenda. He went on, "I doubt that this young lady has the means to fully pay for what Eddie owes you but there has to be something she could offer."

"I doubt it," T-shirt said. "Unless she can suck thousands of dollars' worth of dick in the near future."

Mike felt his blood rise and his fists clench. He looked at Bob who shook his head and smiled sadly. "I'm afraid the young lady is mentally unstable as it is. That's not a viable option."

Mike looked at Glenda who was frowning at Bob.

"Then what?" T-shirt asked.

Bob looked at Glenda. "Glenda, what other income did your husband have besides selling drugs?" he asked.

Mike looked at Glenda. She was staring at Bob blankly. He wondered if she had even heard the question, let alone be able to respond.

"The bar," she said quietly.

"That shithole on Genesee?" T-shirt scoffed. "What the hell would we want with that?"

"I'm sure it's insured," Bob offered.

Now it was T-shirt's turn to frown. He was still considering the bar when Glenda added. "And his VA benefits."

T-shirt thought for another moment then looked at his partner and said, "Wait here, I'm gonna make a call." Then he disappeared into the kitchen.

Mike heard him dial a number and then only bits of one half of the conversation. The evening sun was shining in the front window and the open door making the room feel like an oven. No one moved and the only sound was from the traffic on the thruway.

Finally T-shirt came back with a scrap of paper in his hand. "Okay," he said. "Here's what's going to happen." He looked at Glenda. "Where's the deed to the bar?" he asked.

"Upstairs in a lock box," she answered.

"Go get it."

She did as she was told and came back with a document in her hand. T-shirt took it from her and looked at it. "This is no good," he said. "It's all in Eddie's name."

"I'll sign it," Glenda said. "I've signed Eddie's name for a lot of stuff."

T-shirt looked at his partner who just shrugged. "Hmm, okay, and you'll sign anything else we need?"

"Yes," she answered.

He handed her the scrap paper he was holding. "And the VA checks, you're gonna sign them and send them to this address in Florida."

Glenda looked at the paper and hesitated. She was thinking about something.

"Done," Bob interjected. She finally nodded.

After she forged Eddie's name on the deed for the business the two men left. Bob closed the front door. Mike looked at Glenda and she finally broke down. He put his arm around her but she pulled away. She looked at Bob and said, "What am I going to live on now?"

He shook his head and said, "At least you're going to live."

She clenched her fists and it looked like she was going to scream. She didn't though, she bit it off and hurried upstairs.

Mike and Bob stood for a moment in silence. "I guess I should thank you," Mike finally said.

"For what?"

"For dealing with those guys."

Bob shook his head, "You do whatever you want with that mess. It was my bad luck to walk into the middle of that bullshit."

"What do you mean?" Mike asked, confused.

"I really was looking for you," Bob answered. "I need to talk to you about your father."

THIRTY-NINE

JULY 3, 1988

ONCE THEY CONFIRMED that Shultz was now going by the name Michael Kohler they were able to track him down. His current address, according to the DMV was in the Kensington Village apartments on Cleveland Drive. His last W-2 from the State Department of Taxation listed his employer as a scrap yard on William Street near the city line.

It was shortly after noon when Carl pulled the unmarked Ford into the lot of the scrap yard.

"Shit, I know this asshole." Miller said from the passenger seat.

"Who?"

"The owner of this establishment," Miller added. "I got a call out last month for a break in here. He's an ornery cuss."

Carl pulled up to the front door and was out of the car. He swung the door open and stepped inside the musty office. A heavy-set man was seated on a stool behind the counter. He had a three day growth of stubble on his jowled face and was wearing a filthy ball cap. "That's not a parking space," he grunted. "You're blocking the entrance."

Carl ignored that and pulled out his badge. "Michael Kohler," he said.

"What about him?" the man said.

Carl was growing impatient. "Is he here?"

The man looked at Miller. "I know you," he said. "You're the one who didn't do jack-shit about the break-in."

Carl had lost all patience. He walked up closer to the counter and snapped his fingers in the man's face. "Hey, Junior Samples. Let's focus," he said.

The man stood up, his face turning red. "Who the fuck…" he started.

Carl bent over the counter and interrupted, "We don't have time for this bullshit," he said, his voice rising. "Michael Kohler! Is he here or not?"

"Why, what's he done?"

Carl started to walk around the counter but Miller put his arm out to stop him. Carl recognized a bully and an asshole when he saw one and the urge to grab this guy by his dirty coveralls and give him a good shake was overpowering.

The man pulled a tire iron from under the counter. "Go ahead," Carl growled. "Two outcomes: You hit me and get charged with assaulting a police officer or I take it from you and shove it up your fat ass."

"Carl…" Miller said, trying to sound calm.

"You're a real tough guy, aren't ya?" the man spat. "Got a gun and a badge."

"Yeah, I do have a gun and a badge," Carl said. He took his handcuffs off of his belt. "Turn around."

"The fuck you doing?" the man protested.

"Arresting you for obstructing justice, threatening a peace officer and harboring a fugitive and whatever else I can think of on the way to the station."

The man slowly put the tire iron back under the counter. "He ain't here," he said.

"Michael Kohler?" Carl asked, returning the cuffs to his belt.

"That's who you were asking about, wasn't it?" the man sneered.

"He does work here though, correct?" Miller asked.

The man looked at Miller. "Yep. He left early today."

Shit, Carl thought, not again. He straightened his jacket and looked at the man again. "Listen, Michael Kohler is wanted for questioning in an ongoing investigation and we are going to locate him. Consider yourself warned that any attempt to contact him or warn him will be dealt with severely. If you think I'm joking and we don't find him, I will pull your phone records and personally come back here and jam you up so hard you won't be able to see straight for a year."

"Yeah, whatever," the man said as he sat back down on his stool.

Carl walked back up to the counter and leaned over towards the man. "Part of me hopes that you do something stupid," he said in a low voice.

Back out in the car, Carl had Miller contact Devry and the other detective who were staking out the apartment on Cleveland Drive.

"He's not at work," Miller said into the radio.

"No sign of him here," Devry answered. "We did have an unidentified female enter the apartment at 11:26."

Carl took the mic from Miller and pressed the button. "Just make sure the uniforms are out of sight."

"Copy that," Devry responded. "They're set up around the corner."

"I wonder who the girl is?" Miller asked.

"Yeah, me too," Carl said. Although he had an idea.

MIKE'S MOOD HAD improved slightly. About mid-morning he had had enough of his prick of a boss at the scrap yard. He told him he had a stomach bug and was taking the rest of the day off. The boss bitched of course but what could he do. Not a lot of people were beating down his door to work there. Mike stopped at a payphone and told her he was coming home early and bringing lunch.

He pulled up to the curb in front of the apartment. The smell of hotdogs and French fries from the Ja-Fa-Fa Hots bag was making his mouth water. He was halfway up the walk when he heard a voice behind him.

"Michael Schultz!"

He froze for a moment. Suddenly the sun beating down felt hotter, the air thicker.

"Michael Shultz," the voice called again. He turned in the direction of the voice. It was a stocky, middle-aged man in a rumpled sport coat. He was holding up a badge. There was a younger man in a suit behind him. His coat was open and his right hand was near the butt of a holstered pistol. He heard a sound from the street and when he looked in that direction he saw a sedan and a patrol car there, the occupants getting out.

"Mike? What's going on?" He looked towards the apartment. She was standing in the doorway, barefoot in shorts and a tank top.

"Glenda? Glenda Kolb?" The man who had called out to him was asking her.

She looked confused for a moment but then shook her head. "No!" She protested.

"My name is Debbie Swiatek. What do you want with him?"

"Go back inside, Deb," Mike said. "I'm sure this is all a misunderstanding."

"I don't understand," Debbie said. By now several neighbors and passersby had stopped what they were doing and were gawking at the scene in front of them.

"It's alright, Miss," Carl said. "We just need to ask Mike some questions."

She looked confused again. She looked at Mike and then at Carl. Carl waved the uniforms off and then said to Mike, "Give her the food."

Mike walked up to her and handed her the bag. "It's alright, Deb. Go back inside."

CARL PUT SCHULTZ into the back of the car and they drove wordlessly back to the station on Union Road. Carl was watching him in the rearview mirror, waiting for him to say something or ask a question but Schultz remained silent all the way into the interview room off of the Detective Bureau. Shultz was seated in the room with a uniformed officer standing in the doorway while Carl conferred with Captain D'Agostino, Devry and Miller. Twenty minutes later Carl entered the room and sat down opposite Shultz. He opened the file folder he had brought with him and took out a sheet of paper. He looked across the table at Shultz and tried to get a read on him. The kid just looked back at him impassively. Carl pressed the record button on the tape machine on the table and started; "The time is 13:05, July third, 1988. I am Detective Carl Wisneiwski. I am interviewing Michael Kohler, also known as Michael P. Schultz." He looked up again at Schultz.

"You haven't asked what this is about," Carl said.

"I figured you'd tell me at some point," Shultz replied.

"Alright." Carl looked down at the paper in front of him. "We are investigating the homicide of Arthur Schultz, the date of which we are still trying to establish. Arthur Schultz's remains were found in a chest freezer in the basement of a house at 127 Pinehurst Avenue, Cheektowaga New York." He looked over the top of his reading glasses at Shultz, still no reaction.

He took off his glasses and stared at Schultz. "Mr. Shultz, do you have any information relevant to the death of your father?"

"It's Kohler and shouldn't I have a lawyer?" Schultz asked.

"That is your right Mr. Shultz." Carl replied. "Let me ask you though, do you think you need a lawyer?"

Schultz just stared back at him. "Very well, Mr. Schultz, I mean Kohler." Carl said closing the file. He checked his watch. "Interview terminated at 13:14. It will be resumed once Mr. Kohler is provided with legal counsel. Until that time Mr. Kohler will be detained as a material witness and a flight risk." He saw Schultz's body tense. He reached over and hit the stop button on the recorder, then stood up. He nodded at the uniformed officer standing off to the side who took a set of handcuffs off his belt and approached Schultz.

Carl stepped towards the door and then turned around. "Just curious Mike," he said, "when was the last time you saw your mom?"

Schultz's face darkened but he still remained silent.

FORTY

A FEW DAYS after Alex Chu's thugs had visited, Glenda finished transferring ownership of the bar to another local associate of Chu's. Five weeks later a mysterious fire broke out in the building's basement. An investigation by the County Fire inspector proved inconclusive as to the origin of the fire, the business was shuttered and an insurance settlement was paid out.

Mike's lease for the apartment in Tiorunda ran out that October. With Nick facing jail time for the narcotics charge he moved in with Glenda on a temporary basis. Alex Chu seemed to be placated for the time being and they hadn't heard from him or his associates since the bar had been turned over.

Mike and Glenda usually slept in separate rooms. On more than one occasion they had been intimate though. The first time Mike had just gotten out of the shower and they were talking in the hallway. Glenda was effervescent. Suddenly they were embracing and it happened. Maybe it was the proximity to one another or just the basic human need for contact, but it happened nonetheless. Glenda could be warm and affectionate or sullen and aloof. When she was the former, they formed an easy union that seemed to comfort both of them. When she was in one of her darker moods, Mike cut her a wide swath and let her be.

Bob Czerczak had warned Mike about his father's increasingly troublesome behavior. He was often visibly intoxicated. He could hear Arthur shouting inside the Shultz's house and if he did see him outside he was swearing at the neighbor's kids for some real or imagined transgression.

The day after Christmas, Mike walked around the corner and looked up his parent's driveway. There was no sign of his father's car. He walked up to the front door and rang the bell. A moment later his mother answered the door. It was after noon but she was still in a housecoat and it looked like she had been sleeping. Her hair was pulled back, it was grayer than he remembered it and her eyes looked glassy.

"Michael," she said quietly.

"Hi mom," he said. She didn't move to let him in. It was cold though and he didn't want her standing in the December chill. He gently put a hand on her shoulder and eased past her into the living room.

He looked around the room. It was the day after Christmas but you wouldn't have known it. No tree, no decorations. His mother used to love Christmas. He realized that it had been part of her struggle to make the family seem normal.

He handed her the wrapped box, a scarf he had bought at the mall a few days before to use as a premise to drop by. She looked at it for a moment seemingly confused and then smiled slightly.

"Where is he?" Mike asked.

She looked at him and then it registered what he was asking. "Upstairs," she said quietly.

"Where's the car?" He asked.

She looked down at the box in her hand and cringed.

"Mom?

"Impounded."

Mike shook his head. "Why?"

"DWI," she answered in a near whisper.

They heard a stirring from upstairs. His mother looked at him and said, "Michael, you should go."

He couldn't stand it though. The thought of his mother living like this with an unapologetic, abusive asshole. He stood his ground.

A moment later his father came down the stairs wearing a dingy undershirt and work pants. His hair was unruly and he had a five day growth of stubble. He stopped halfway down the stairs and took in the scene in front of him.

"What are you doing here?" he growled.

"I came to see Mom," Mike answered flatly.

Arthur walked the rest of the way down the stairs. He shot Mary a dirty look and then fixed his bloodshot eyes on Mike. "You know you're not welcome here," he said.

"You can't stop me from seeing my mother."

"My house, my rules," Arthur hissed.

Mike took a step closer to his father. "Well, fuck you and your rules."

Arthur's face turned red. "You goddamned punk!" He went to slap Mike across the face but Mike caught him by the wrist and pushed Art backwards into the bannister. Arthur grunted and straightened up. "Stop!" he heard his mother scream. Arthur's eyes were wild and he rushed at Mike. Mike knocked Arthur's arms down and put him in a headlock. Arthur was struggling with all his strength now. They lurched a few feet and Mike lost his balance when his leg hit the coffee table. They fell over the table and it gave way beneath them with a loud crack. Mike rolled on top and pinned his father down on the shattered wood. He heard the front door open.

"You fucking punk!" Arthur spat. "I always knew you were an ungrateful little bastard."

Mike put a hand on his father's throat, effectively silencing him. "Grateful for what?" he asked, staring into his father's eyes. "An alcoholic father who beats him and his mother? A father who never accepts the blame for any of the shitty things he's done?"

Art grunted and it sounded like he was choking. Mike eased the pressure in his father's throat. Art gasped, took a breath and then spat in Mike's face. Mike, was blind with rage, he pulled back his right hand and punched his father hard in the mouth. The brief satisfaction Mike felt was soon replaced by a sharp pain in his hand. He had cut his knuckle on his father's teeth.

Arthur was dazed and his mouth was bleeding. He started to struggle again and Mike renewed the pressure he was using to pin him down. The sound of the front door opening again and heavy footsteps. Mike felt a strong pair of hands on his shoulder and the collar of his jacket as he was pulled off of his father.

It was Bob Czerczak. He pulled Mike to his feet and then stood in front of him. "That's enough," he said. Art rolled off the broken table onto his side and spat out blood. Mary was standing off to the side, looking distressed and near tears.

Czerczak gently backed Mike up to the door and waited until Mike was looking at him. "Get out of here," he said firmly. "I'll take care of it."

Mike took a look at his father and then his mother. As badly as he wanted to finish kicking the old man's ass, he realized it would only make things worse.

FORTY-ONE
JULY 5, 1988

CAPTAIN D'AGOSTINO WAS nervous. They had Michael Kohler/Shultz in custody but still hadn't charged him with anything. Shultz had been offered access to a public defender but he had quietly declined and arranged for an attorney of his own. Because the next day was a holiday, the lawyer finally showed up on the fifth.

The lawyer, a fifty-something criminal attorney from Amherst came in guns blazing, demanding that Shultz be released immediately since he hadn't been charged. He was appeased when D'Agostino relented after conferring with Carl and all parties agreed to one final interview before Shultz could be set free.

Carl and Devry spent a frustrating hour with Shultz and his attorney. Shultz gave up nothing, the lawyer often interrupting and claiming that Shultz had nothing to do with the demise of his father. Carl was reaching his breaking point.

"If I understand what you're saying, or not saying," Carl said. "You didn't kill your father."

Shultz looked at his attorney who subtly nodded. "No, I didn't," he answered.

Carl was ready to reach across the table and choke the kid. He was trying to control his breathing. Then Devry chimed in, "Michael, what did you see?"

Another glance between Shultz and the lawyer. No reaction from either. The room was silent until Bill Miller knocked on the

---

203

door and stuck his head in. "Carl, you have a call on three," he said.

"Take a message," Carl answered curtly.

"He said it's important," Miller replied, not backing down.

Carl turned in his seat and looked at Miller. He gestured towards the table with Schultz and his attorney as if to ask: What could be more important than this?

Miller simply added, "You're going to want to take this."

Carl stood up. The lawyer immediately spoke up, "I take it this interview is over and my client is free to go."

Carl was headed to the door. He looked over his shoulder and said, "Just give me a goddamn minute, okay?"

A minute later he was at his desk. He picked up the receiver and punched the button for line three.

"Detective Wisneiwski," he said.

Silence on the line and then a familiar voice. "Carl?"

"Bob?" Carl could feel his heart beat in his chest. "Where are you?"

"Never mind that," Bob slurred.

"What do you want Bob?"

"The kid didn't do it," Czerczak answered.

"Jesus Christ, Bob…"

"Art Schultz was a piece of shit." Czerczak hesitated. "I know that doesn't matter in the big picture. But the kid's innocent."

"Bob, I know you know a lot more than you told me…" Carl started, but then he heard a click and the line went dead. He stood for a moment with the receiver in his hand. Then he hung up and punched in the number for the desk Sergeant.

He returned to the interview room where the others were waiting expectantly. He looked at the lawyer and said, "Your client is free to go."

The lawyer stood up. "Well thanks for that," he huffed. "And just so you know, we will be considering a suit for wrongful arrest and detention."

Carl fixed his gaze on Mike Schultz. "Whatever," he said. "In the meantime, please advise your client to make himself available until this investigation is concluded." He tried again to get a read on Schultz but got nothing.

"Let's go," the lawyer said. Schultz stood up and followed his attorney out of the room.

"What's going on?"

It took a moment for Carl to realize that Devry was talking to him. "We have a potential witness," he answered.

"Who would that be?" Devry asked standing up.

Carl looked at Devry, hesitated for a moment and then said, "A neighbor, Robert Czerzak."

"And he cleared Schultz?"

"Potentially," Carl answered.

They were face to face now. Devry clicked his pen and returned it to his jacket pocket. "You know, Carl," he said, "I can't help you if you're holding back on something relevant to the case."

Carl looked him in the eye. "I know," he answered. "And I know this hasn't been exactly by the book. I think we're close though and there's something I need to check out."

Devry pursed his lips and then said, "Okay, do what you need to do. I'm not crazy about it but for some reason I trust you. Just don't shut me out totally. I'm here to help."

Carl nodded and left the room.

FORTY-TWO
MAY 12, 1985

As Bob Czerczak was getting out of his car he glanced across the street and noticed that the Schultz's storm door was hanging open. He briefly thought about ignoring it. His late wife, Patty, would have told him that he wasn't a cop anymore and he should mind his own business. His curiosity got the better of him and he walked across the street. The house was deathly silent as he approached the front door. As he got closer he saw that the storm door had been partially pulled off its hinges. He stepped up onto the stoop and peered inside. An end table was knocked over and the lamp that had been on it was lying broken on the floor. It wasn't until he stepped inside that he heard a low moaning sound coming from the kitchen.

He walked into the kitchen and saw Mary Shultz seated at the table holding a dishrag over her face.

"Mary," he said quietly.

She pulled the towel off her face and looked up suddenly. Her left eye was almost swollen shut. She winced and put the towel back on her face.

Bob could feel his blood starting to boil. "Where is he?" he asked.

Mary just shook her head. Bob walked over and sat down across from her. He tried to take the anger out of his voice. "Mary, I've seen this kind of thing before. The first thing you have to understand is that this isn't your fault." She sobbed and used the towel to wipe the tears from her cheeks. "I've lived across the street from you for years now and I've watched your husband turn into a very angry man. I know Michael and I know that Art pushed him away and won't let him near you."

She was shaking her head and trying to stifle her crying. Bob was starting to wonder if she was listening.

"Mary, this is only going to get worse."

She looked down. She seemed totally defeated. "Let me take you to Michael," he said.

Her expression changed somewhat, her features less contorted. She looked up at him with a mix of fear and surrender.

FORTY-THREE
JULY 5- JULY 6, 1988

Aᴄᴛᴇʀ Mɪᴋᴇ Sᴄʜᴜʟᴛᴢ was released, the team was told to report to Captain D'Agostino's office. When Carl arrived, the door
to D'Agostino's office was shut and Miller and Devry were waiting
outside. Carl got Miller's attention and gave him a 'what's going on'
look. Miller just shrugged in return.

A moment later the door swung open and Chief Kopasz walked
briskly past without acknowledging any of them. Devry went into
the Captain's office first followed by Miller and Carl. D'Agostino
was sitting behind his desk signing papers. He didn't look up or
ask anyone to sit down. "Chief Kopasz is requesting further assis-
tance from the Sheriff's Office and the State Police," he said. He
finished his signature and looked up. "After today he feels that
we're no closer to solving this than we were before." He looked
from one man to the other, as if waiting for someone to protest.
The room was quiet. His eyes lingered on Carl for a moment.

Carl returned his stare and tried to remain impassive. He'd been
waiting for the day when the Chief would lose patience and pull
the plug. Hitting a brick wall with Schultz must have been the last
straw. D'Agostino went on. "When the detectives arrive tomorrow
I want copies of all the files and notes we have ready to go." He
paused and waited again for someone to say something, still nothing was said. "Okay, that's it," he finished.

Carl was the first one out of the office. He had his orders but he didn't care. He felt like he was close now. Part of him realized he should tell the Captain and Devry what he was up to, but he didn't want to do that until he was sure this time. As angry as he was at Bob Czerczak for giving him the runaround, he wanted to give him a chance to explain himself. He went down the hall to the dispatch office and went in.

Marty Gould, the plump, forty-something dispatch supervisor was seated at his desk. He held up a piece of paper when he saw Carl enter. "I got it, but I'm not sure if it's going to make you happy."

After Bob Czerczak's cryptic phone call, Carl had asked Gould to trace the number. Carl looked at the handwritten note Gould had given him. There was an address and a phone number. "206 area code?" Carl asked.

"Fort Erie, Ontario," Gould answered. "It took a while but I got through to Bell Canada and they informed me that it belongs to a pay phone at that address."

"Shit," Carl said. In reality, he knew that Czerczak wouldn't call from where he was actually staying. He thought about something he'd seen at Czerczak's house weeks before.

"Sorry Carl," Gould said.

"Don't worry about it Marty," Carl responded. "This actually might help."

He went home and waited. He resisted the urge to take the bourbon out of the cupboard and turned the TV on instead. He idly flipped through the channels for a while until he settled on a Yankees game. He wasn't really watching it, he was thinking about the events of the last few weeks. The investigation would be taken out of his hands tomorrow but that didn't really bother him. In a few months, he would be another retired cop with too much time on his hands and too many stories that nobody really cared about. If this was the thing he would be remembered by then so be it.

The sun went down outside his apartment window but he waited still. Finally at ten o'clock he got up, went to his bedroom and changed into a dark t-shirt and jeans. Fifteen minutes later he parked his car at the end of Evergreen Place. He got out of the car and looked around. It was quiet. He walked around the corner and up Bob Czerczak's driveway.

The neighbor's house was dark. Fortunately there were no windows on the side of the house next to Czerczak's. He walked to the side of Czercak's garage and forced the man door open with a pry bar. It opened with a loud crack. Wasting no time, he stepped inside the dark garage, closed the door and looked back out through the dirty window. Satisfied that no had witnessed him break and enter a retiree's home, he pulled the flashlight out of his back pocket and turned it on.

From the garage, he entered the kitchen. The house was closed and stuffy. He walked into the living room and over to Bob's chair. He picked up the picture he had seen the first time he had talked to Bob. Czerczak and his then teenaged son were standing on a small dock, each one of them holding up a fish on a line. Carl returned the picture to the table and went down the hallway. The first room he checked was obviously Czerczak's bedroom. The bed was somewhat made. Given Bob's condition that was to be expected. He had still put more effort into it than Carl usually did.

The second room had probably been the son's at one time, but had been converted into an office. The walls were covered with commendations from Czerczak's time as a policeman, family pictures and a large mounted fish.

Carl's eyes fell on the desk on the other side of the room. He sat down and turned on the desk lamp. He pulled open the desk's file drawer and started thumbing through the tabs on the folders, insurance papers, pension information and all the other important scraps of personal information one collects in a lifetime. Towards the back of the drawer he found what he was looking for, a file marked *Crystal Beach.*

Back at his apartment he called information and got the number for the Fort Erie Ontario Police Department. He called and was informed that Crystal Beach was outside of their purview and fell under the jurisdiction of the Ontario Provincial Police, the Canadian equivalent of the State Police. He was given a number, called it and identified himself. He explained to the duty Sergeant that Bob Czerczak was a material witness in a homicide and that a warrant was being prepared to bring him back to the States. The Sergeant was hesitant at first, explaining to Carl that this was more a matter for the RCMP. Carl said that it would all be done by the book the next day, but for now all he wanted was confirmation that Czerczak was at the cottage that Carl had found the deed for at Czerczak's house. The Sergeant said he would see what he could do and call Carl back.

Carl hung up the phone. He wondered if he was getting the brush off. Maybe he should just jump in his car and head over the border now. It was after eleven and a forty minute drive to Crystal Beach. He was exhausted. He decided to stay put and hope the OPP would do him this favor.

He sat in his recliner and closed his eyes. Before he knew it he was asleep. At some point the phone rang, he wasn't sure how long he'd been out for, but he leapt to his feet and picked up the phone in the kitchen on the third ring.

"Detective Wisniewski?" the voice on the other end asked.

"Yeah," Carl responded, clearing his throat.

"It's Sergeant O'Rourke. As far as we can tell, your man is there."

"That's great." He'd asked the Sergeant if they could be discreet before and followed up with; "Did your people see him or speak to him?"

"No," O'Rourke said curtly. "We know what discreet means. I can't say I'm happy about all this clandestine stuff."

"I understand," Carl answered. "I appreciate you doing this. I promise you tomorrow we'll have all of our i's dotted and our t's crossed."

"Fine," O'Rourke said. He added a short goodbye and hung up.

Carl looked at the clock on the kitchen wall, it was after three. He needed a few hours of sleep before he did what he needed to do next.

THE DROUGHT ENDED that morning. Carl had woken up at 6:30 a.m. and was now driving through sheets of rain towards the Peace Bridge. He cleared customs on the Canadian side and was in Crystal Beach forty minutes later.

Using a map he had picked up at a gas station, he found his way to Crystal Beach Drive, a narrow, tree-lined street that ran along the Northern Shore of Lake Erie. The rain had fogged his windows, so he was driving at a crawl down the street, looking at house numbers. He almost passed the small, unassuming cottage. There was an older Buick in the drive with New York plates. He pulled over and climbed out. The rain had eased some, but it was still falling steadily in big drops. His shirt was soaked by the time he got to the door to knock. There was no answer so after a minute he walked past the Buick to a chain link gate that he pushed open to reveal a gravel covered path to the back of the property. When he got to the back of the house he found himself standing on a patch of rough grass that led to a small beach and then the expanse of Lake Erie beyond that.

He looked in the rear window into a small kitchen. There was a coffee cup on the counter and a jacket thrown over a stool. He walked up onto a small wooden porch and the back door of the cottage and knocked. He waited again, the only sound coming from the rain splattering down on the lake behind him. He put his hand on the door latch and pulled the door open.

"Bob!" he called out. Nothing. He walked into the kitchen area, dripping rain water onto the floor. The house was eerily quiet. It was small inside, it looked like just a kitchen, living room, bedroom and bath. "Bob," he called out again. Carl was just about to head to the bedroom when he saw a piece of paper and an envelope on the kitchen counter. He picked it up and saw a note written in an unsteady hand. The first line read; *To whom it may concern...* There was an envelope under the page that Carl saw was addressed to him. He scanned the next few lines of the note. "Shit," Carl said out loud. He looked out the kitchen window towards the lake. There was a small dock. It was empty but there was one line hanging forlornly off of one of the posts.

He burst through the door and sprinted across the sand out onto the dock. He rubbed the rain out of his eyes and peered out across the water. Nothing but gray, the sky, the rain and the lake almost indistinguishable from one another. Finally he saw it, about thirty yards off shore, a small boat riding low in the water. Carl squinted and saw that the boat was unoccupied and there wasn't a soul in sight anywhere near it either.

"Fuck," he screamed. He turned around and looked up and down the beach, there was no one in sight. He ran back to the cottage and through the back door. He tore through all four rooms but didn't find a phone. He ran out the front door over to the neighbor's house and pounded on the door until a nervous looking woman in a bathrobe answered. He pulled out his badge and told her to call the police.

Ten minutes later a patrol car arrived from the OPP. A short time after that an OPP patrol boat had arrived and was circling the water around the abandoned row boat. Two more cars arrived, a uniformed Lieutenant in one of them.

Carl was given a towel to dry himself off and sat in a chair at the kitchen table while the cops came in and out, making calls on their radios and looking the place over.

"No sign of him yet," the lieutenant said.

Carl just looked up and nodded.

"You're Carl Wisniewski?" the Lieutenant asked. The name Forbes was on his brass name tag.

"Yeah." Carl saw that Forbes was holding the envelope that had been addressed to him.

Forbes looked at the envelope and then back at Carl. "Not much in the note he left," he said. "I suppose this is related?"

"Yeah, probably."

"And you knew Mr. Czerczak?"

"We used to work together."

Forbes thought for a moment and then reached into the pocket of his raincoat and pulled out another pair of latex gloves. He handed the gloves to Carl. "I'm going to let you open it, but be advised we're going to keep it as evidence until the inquiry." He handed the envelope to Carl.

Carl looked at the envelope, turned it over and ripped it open. There was a letter, written in the same unsteady hand as Bob's suicide note.

> *Carl,*
> *I saw the OPP boys casing the place last night and*

knew you probably wouldn't be far behind.

I am responsible for the death of Arthur Schultz.

While I have some regrets about what happened, be sure that Art Schulz was a piece of shit. Not that it excuses what I did, but the man was an unrepentant alcoholic abuser. What he did to his family was inexcusable. While I admit I'm far from the one who should stand in judgment of another man, I'm not sorry that he's gone.

My main regret is that I didn't do something sooner. His wife is an innocent victim of a truly bad situation.

His death was an accident, but I'm the one who caused it. We got into a fight and he fell over and split his head open on a kitchen counter. Looking back now, I realize I should have followed my better instincts and called it in. At the time though, for reasons I can't explain, I panicked and tried to cover it up. I was trying to help Mary and the kid. We were going to move the body but then the stroke happened and we just kept putting it off. I tried to take care of her the best I could but she turned in on herself and things just got worse. I even posed as her husband when she sold the house. In the end she wouldn't open the door for me or her son. I suppose the biggest regret I have is that I let her down.

I saw on the news that you had Mike Schultz in custody. He may be a witness or even an accessory but he didn't do it. If anything he's just collateral damage from his asshole father

I didn't know you all that well when we worked together but you seem like a good cop. I'm sorry I didn't tell you the truth right away, I just needed to figure some things out.

It's funny, but I always tried to do the right thing. Now at the end I really put my foot in it. I hope you or anyone else don't make the same mistakes I did.

That's it.

Bob C.

Carl let the letter fall into his lap. He felt totally drained. He looked up when he heard the back door open.

A young constable took half a step inside, jerked a thumb over his shoulder towards the lake and said, "Lieutenant, they've got something."

FORTY-FOUR

JUNE 12, 1985

Bob had finally coaxed Mary Schultz out of her house and they made their way around the corner to the house on Pinehurst as a light rain started to fall. Glenda answered the door and stared at them for a moment and then finally let them in. Mike came downstairs and looked at the state his mother was in.

"Mom?" he said.

Mary glanced at him and then looked down. Glenda walked over and touched Mary on the arm and then gently led her over to the couch.

Bob looked at Mike who was becoming visibly more agitated by the moment but obviously trying to hold it in for his mother's sake. Finally he grabbed his jacket off the bannister and headed towards the back of the house. Bob followed him through the kitchen and out the back door.

"Hey," Bob said. Mike didn't seem to hear him and walked to the back of his car.

"Michael," Bob said. Mike had popped the trunk and pulled out a tire iron. "Stop!" Bob said firmly.

Mike turned towards Bob, his eyes burning. "I'm going to fucking kill him," he growled.

Bob walked up to Mike and looked him in the eye. "The hell you are," he said. "What good will you be to your mom if you're locked up?"

Mike was shaking his head. "I don't care," he said. "You have no idea what it's ..." his voice trailed off.

Bob put one hand on his shoulder and another on the tire iron. "I don't son," he said quietly, "but now is not the time to go running off half-cocked. The best thing we can do is get her out of there and let the law deal with your dad."

Mike looked skeptical, but the fight had gone out of him. He loosened his grip on the tire iron and Bob took it.

"Your mom's going to need some things, a toothbrush . . . maybe something to help her sleep." Can you get those things for her?"

Mike nodded but then asked, "What if he comes for her?"

"I'm going home to make a call to the station," Bob answered. "I'll keep an eye on the old man."

Mike stood for a moment, unsure what to do. Finally he turned and headed to the driver's side door.

"Call me when you get back," Bob added. He walked back into the house.

Glenda was in the kitchen. She looked at Bob and then the tire iron in his hand. "Where is he going?" she asked nervously.

Bob realized he still had the iron in his hand and then set it down on the counter. "He just went to pick up a few things."

"He's not going back to the house is he?"

"No, no" Bob answered. "How is she?" he asked nodding towards the living room.

Glenda frowned and shook her head, "Not good. She won't talk or answer me when I talk to her. It's like she totally shut down."

Bob nodded and said, "Okay. I need you to look after her for a while. I'm going to my house to make a call and keep an eye out for the husband."

Bob walked quickly back to his house. He looked at the Schultz's; still no sign of Art. He called the number he knew by heart for the Cheektowaga Police. Whoever he spoke to at first didn't seem to recognize Bob's name or even care that he was retired CPD. Bob asked to speak to the Captain on duty but was told that the Captain was in a meeting and couldn't be disturbed. Finally he was connected with a Sergeant who seemed to be listening at least.

"And the husband isn't at the house right now?" the Sergeant asked.

Bob had already told him that. They were wasting time. "Yes, for Christ's sake," he snapped.

"Sir, I'm only trying to get the information we need," the Sergeant snapped back.

Jesus Christ, Bob thought. Thirty-seven years on the job and now being treated like any other old crank who called in to complain about the neighbor's dog shitting on their lawn.

"Look, you sanctimonious fuck," he said, "just get a car out here." He slammed the receiver down. He stood for a minute looking at the phone and then remembered what he was supposed to be doing. He went into his home office and looked out the window across the street. Art Schultz's rusted Buick was in the driveway.

"Shit," Bob said to himself. He stared at the Schultz's house. It was starting to get dark out and there were no lights on, just the car parked crookedly in the driveway and the front storm door hanging off its hinges. He went to his front door and outside. He walked quickly across the street and up the front walk. He listened by the front door. The only sound was the rain which had started coming down harder. He pushed the door open and slowly stepped inside. The only light on in the house was coming from the kitchen. He stepped into the kitchen. Art wasn't there, but an open bottle of cheap whiskey sat on the table. "Shit," he said again.

GLENDA WAS STANDING in the doorway between her kitchen and the living room, looking at Mike's mother. She had offered her water, tea, anything she needed but Mary had barely responded. The back door opened behind her. Thank God Mike was back.

She turned around but it wasn't Mike. Art Schultz was standing in the doorway, wild-eyed and rain soaked.

"Get out of my house!" Glenda said.

"Where is she?" Art slurred.

"She's not here."

"Bullshit!" he roared. He lurched forward a step. "I know the little creep was shacked up over here with you. I know he'd bring her here."

"Get the fuck out of my house!" Glenda yelled. She took a step towards Art.

"Get out of the way, whore!" Art said. He went to push Glenda but she knocked his arm aside and slapped him hard on the side of his face. He reeled for a second and then grabbed her by the shoulders. With her arms pinned to her sides, her only recourse was to bring her knee up. Despite Art's condition, he anticipated it and turned aside. Her knee connected with his thigh. She could feel him using their momentum as he threw her into the kitchen table. Her back hit the table first, knocking the wind out of her. She collapsed to the floor, gasping for air.

"Stay down, you filthy cunt," Art spat. He straightened up and walked into the living room.

Mary barely looked up at her husband. Her eyes were vacant, glassy and seemingly resigned to her fate. Art walked over to where she was sitting and stood over her. "Get up," he said.

She didn't move. She looked down into her lap and her shoulders drooped. "I said get up!" He bellowed. He bent over and grabbed her by the wrists.

Before he could pull Mary to her feet, Glenda brought the tire iron down onto the back of Art's head. There was a loud *crack*, then Art grunted and fell forward on top of Mary. He rolled off and landed on his back on the floor. His bloodshot eyes were staring up at nothing and the blood was already pooling around his head.

Glenda stood panting, wincing from the pain in her ribs. Mary was looking at Glenda, her face slack. Slowly, slowly then she leaned over and looked at her husband on the floor in front of her and her face contorted. She made a gasping sound and seemed to stop breathing.

Just then someone tried the front door. It was locked so whoever it was started pounding on the door. Neither Glenda nor Mary moved. The pounding stopped and a moment later Bob rushed into the room from the kitchen. He surveyed the scene and walked over to Glenda.

"Easy girl," he said, gently taking the tire iron from her. He pulled her a few steps back from the couch. They heard the sound of the back door opening again and Mike was in the room. He stared, mouth agape at his father's body.

Slowly, Mary lowered herself off the couch until she was kneeling next to Art. She let out a sob and then put her hands on his face.

"Mary," Bob said. He walked over and stood over her. "Mary," he said again.

She let out another sob and then looked up at Bob and then at Glenda. She started to scream then, an animalistic howl.

Everyone stood for a moment in disbelief. Bob finally looked at Mike, pointed at Glenda and said. "Get her out of here!"

Mike didn't respond. He was still staring at his father's body. "Mike!" Bob yelled.

Mike looked at him blankly but didn't answer.

"I'll take care of this," Bob said. "Just get her out of here."

Mike finally walked over to Glenda, put his arm around her shoulders and quietly led her out of the room. Mary had stopped shrieking. Bob was able to pull her off of Art's body and get her back on the couch where she curled into a fetal position and started to sob softly. Bob heard the sound of Mike's car starting in the driveway and looked around the room. He knew he should call it in. What about the girl though? He looked down at Art Schultz and felt nothing even close to pity for him. He had to think now, he needed time.

He dragged Art's body down to the basement, wrapped it in a plastic drop cloth and then dropped it into the freezer. What was he doing? Had he lost his mind? No, somehow this felt right, it felt like justice. He cursed and went back upstairs.

Mary was still on the couch. She was quiet now and seemed to be barely breathing. He took a blanket off of the recliner and covered her up.

He found a bucket and some rags under the kitchen sink and used it to clean up the blood on the living room floor and then the trail that led through the kitchen.

When he finished, he was covered in sweat and exhausted. Now what? He decided to go home and clean himself up. Then he would come back and watch over Mary until he figured out what to do next. Walking home, he felt light-headed and then experienced a sharp pain behind his left eye. Had they dispatched a unit after his call to the station? There was no sign of the cops anywhere. He was halfway up his driveway when he felt the entire side of his body constrict with pain. He couldn't breath and was losing his balance. He collapsed a few feet from his front door.

FORTY-FIVE
JULY 8, 1988

CARL WISNIEWSKI SAT at his desk in the otherwise deserted squad room staring at the notebook and a small pile of papers on his desk.

The case was all but closed. The DA had taken Bob Czerczak's suicide note and the letter to Carl into evidence and was preparing a statement. Captain D'Agostino had chewed Carl a new one for going rogue and keeping the rest of the team in the dark about Czerczak's involvement, but in the end was satisfied with the results. Jeff Devry simply shook his hand and wished him good luck. Carl was trying to get a read on Devry but then he realized he just didn't care what the other man thought of him.

Michael Shultz had been brought in with his attorney for another interview and this time proved to be quite chatty. He confirmed Czerczak's version of events with the caveat that he arrived at the house after the deed had been done.

The Kolbs were the only loose end. Schultz had confirmed that Eddie had skipped town after running afoul of his Canadian connection and he stated that Glenda had disappeared the night that his father had been killed. Chief Kopasz had initiated a search for the Kolbs with the understanding that in his eyes, the case wasn't dependent on locating them. He was satisfied that they had their man and was ready to put the case to bed.

Carl pulled the stack of papers closer. It was his retirement paperwork. He had gotten as far as filling out the first few lines; name, badge number, date of hire. He was thinking about Bob Czerczak. He had been thinking about Czerczak a lot the past few days. How sad is it that a guy like Bob would go out that way? Living alone and forgotten about. His last act doing something that he thought was right, but in the end just making an unholy mess of things. Carl wondered if he was headed down the same path. He was already living alone and would be leaving a fraction of the legacy that Czerczak had. He opened the top desk drawer and stuffed the paperwork and his notebook inside. He stood up, pulled off his tie and walked out of the squad room.

Epilogue
July 11, 1988

He pushed open the door to the Bakery on Clinton Street. He was going to bring donuts to work as a peace offering. He was going to give his two weeks' notice at the scrap yard today and his boss, a true prick in the best of times, was probably going to be less than pleased. If there was a scene, he would simply tell the boss to shove the donuts up his fat ass. He didn't care really; he'd found a better job at a collision shop on Broadway.

She was behind the counter, just finishing cashing out an old woman wearing what looked like a housecoat with her hair up in rollers. She looked up, saw him and smiled slightly. 'Hey," she said.

He hadn't seen her in about six months. It looked like she had put a little weight on in the interim. She looked good though, her eyes were clear and she had color in her cheeks.

"Hi," he answered. "Um, a dozen assorted please."

She nodded and took a box off of the rear counter and folded it into shape. "How's Debbie?" she asked.

"Good," he answered. "She got a job at a daycare place. She's thinking of going back to school."

"Nice," she said. She was skillfully packing the box with pastries.

"How are you?" he asked.

"I'm okay. Oh, I did find out I'm bi-polar, so there is that."

He raised his eyebrows. She saw his expression and smiled again. "It's a good thing though," she added. "The doctor said if it's treated it will help with the mood swings."

She finished packing the box and taped it closed. They walked over to the register and he looked at her again. "It's over," he said.

She looked down pensively and then rang in the order. "I know. I saw it in the paper."

He nodded and pulled a five out of his wallet. She handed him his change and they stood for a moment looking at each other.

"You sure you're okay?" he asked.

She thought for a moment and then answered, "I think so. I'm better than I was, I know that."

"Well, thanks," Mike said, holding up the box. He turned to leave.

"What about you?" she said.

He turned around and looked at her. "Yeah," he nodded. "I guess I'm okay. Kinda like you said, better than I was,"

LATER THAT DAY, Mary Schultz was sitting in the day room of the nursing home watching TV. There were a handful of other residents in the room, more than a few of them sound asleep. A young man walked up and stood in front of her. He was holding a small bouquet of flowers.

She looked up at his face and a flicker of recognition showed in her eyes.

"Hi mom."

ACKNOWLEDGMENTS

To Cynthia Lehman, for once again editing the mess I sent you. To my daughter Liz and my wife Jeanne for your proofreading and feedback. I may be defensive and stubborn, but your input is invaluable. To my daughter Emily and for your love and support. To my brothers and sisters for your love and encouragement. To Sara Murello, a talented and very patient artist, for the cover design. And a special thank you to all who read the *Donovan Series*.